How Lincoln, Johnson & The Roosevelts Became President

The Journey Of Four Bright Kids On The Path Of Leadership | Timeless Leadership Lessons

Asher Beaumont Kearns

Hazel Goodwin Hayes

Ivy Doris Skyler

Dedication

To the dreamers, the doers, and the determined—those who see challenges as opportunities and setbacks as stepping stones. May the stories of these four presidents inspire you to lead with courage, compassion, and conviction, no matter where your path may lead.

Table Of Contents

Introduction: Four Presidents, One Nation

The Enduring Lessons of Lincoln, Johnson, and the Roosevelts

In times of national uncertainty, we often look to the past for guidance. The stories of great leaders who faced overwhelming challenges can offer us hope, wisdom, and practical strategies for addressing our own problems. This book focuses on four such leaders: Abraham Lincoln, Lyndon B. Johnson, Theodore Roosevelt, and Franklin D. Roosevelt. These presidents, each facing their own set of monumental challenges, shaped the course of American history and left legacies that continue to influence our nation today.

Why These Four?

You might wonder, "Why these particular presidents?" The answer lies in the remarkable parallels between the issues they faced and those we struggle with today. From civil rights and economic inequality to the proper role of government and America's place on the world stage, the challenges of their eras echo loudly in our current political discourse.

Abraham Lincoln led the nation through its bloodiest conflict, preserving the Union and setting the stage for the eventual abolition of slavery. His leadership during this existential crisis offers valuable insights into managing deep national divisions and upholding democratic principles under extreme pressure.

Lyndon B. Johnson, despite his controversial handling of the Vietnam War, pushed through landmark civil rights legislation and launched ambitious social programs aimed at reducing poverty and inequality. His presidency provides lessons on effecting significant social change and tackling the intricate interplay between domestic and foreign policy.

Theodore Roosevelt, the youngest person to assume the presidency, brought a new energy to the office. His efforts to check the power of big business, conserve natural resources, and assert America's global influence resonate with many of today's hotly debated issues.

Franklin D. Roosevelt guided the nation through two of its greatest challenges: the Great Depression and World War II. His bold approach to government intervention in the economy and his wartime leadership offer valuable perspectives on crisis management and the expansion of presidential power.

Learning from the Past, Leading in the Present

By examining the lives and presidencies of these four leaders, we gain more than just historical knowledge. We acquire a deeper understanding of leadership itself - how it's forged, how it adapts to challenges, and how it can shape the course of a nation.

This book aims to do more than simply recount historical events. Its goal is to extract timeless principles of leadership from these presidencies and apply them to our current national challenges. How did these leaders approach decision-making in times of crisis? How did they build coalitions and overcome opposition? How did they communicate their vision to the American people? And most importantly, what can today's leaders - and citizens - learn from their successes and failures?

From Humble Beginnings to the White House

One of the most striking aspects of these four presidencies is the diverse backgrounds from which these men rose to power.

Lincoln's journey from a log cabin in Kentucky to the White House is perhaps the most famous "rags-to-riches" story in American political history. Johnson grew up in the hardscrabble Hill Country of Texas, while the two Roosevelts came from a privileged New York family.

These varied backgrounds shaped their worldviews and their approaches to governance. Lincoln's experiences with poverty and hard work informed his belief in the dignity of labor and the importance of economic opportunity. Johnson's childhood experiences with poverty fueled his passion for social reform.

Theodore Roosevelt's wealthy upbringing, combined with his later experiences in the American West, led to his unique blend of progressivism and rugged individualism. Franklin Roosevelt's privileged background didn't prevent him from becoming a champion of the common man during the Great Depression.

By tracing the paths these "bright kids" took to the presidency, we can gain insights into how leaders are formed and how early experiences shape later actions and policies.

Bridging the Gap: Historical Wisdom for Modern Challenges

As we explore the lives and presidencies of these four leaders, we'll constantly draw connections to our current political and social landscape. How might Lincoln's approach to national unity inform our handling of today's partisan divides? What can Johnson's Great Society teach us about addressing persistent poverty and inequality? How might Theodore Roosevelt's "Square Deal" inform current debates about corporate power and environmental protection? What lessons can we draw from Franklin Roosevelt's handling of economic crisis and global conflict?

These questions are not merely academic. They have real-world implications for how we approach governance and citizenship in the 21st century. By understanding how these presidents tackled the challenges of their day, we can better equip ourselves to address the challenges of our own time.

A Nation at Crossroads

The title of this book refers to America as "a nation at crossroads," and indeed, many feel that we are at a critical juncture in our history. We face significant challenges: political polarization, economic inequality, racial tensions, climate change, and questions about America's role in a rapidly changing world order.

In many ways, these challenges echo those faced by Lincoln, Johnson, and the Roosevelts. Lincoln confronted a nation literally torn apart by fundamental disagreements about the nature of the Union and the future of slavery. Johnson battled with the unfinished business of civil rights and sought to build a "Great Society" free from poverty and racial injustice. Theodore Roosevelt tried to balance the interests of business and labor while also asserting America's place on the world stage. Franklin Roosevelt had to restore faith in American democracy and capitalism in the face of global economic collapse and the rise of totalitarianism.

By studying how these presidents approached their own crossroads, we can gain valuable perspectives on how to approach ours.

The Power of Biography

There's a reason why biographies consistently top bestseller lists and why historical figures continue to capture our imagination.

Stories of real people facing real challenges speak to us on a deep, human level. They inspire us, teach us, and sometimes warn us.

This book uses the power of biography to illuminate larger historical trends and extract leadership lessons. We'll get to know these presidents as people - their strengths, their flaws, their doubts, and their triumphs. We'll see how they grew and changed in office, how they handled setbacks, and how they seized opportunities.

Through their stories, we'll gain a richer understanding of American history and the nature of presidential leadership. But more than that, we'll gain insights that can inform our own lives and our own engagement with the political process.

A Roadmap for the Book

In the chapters that follow, we'll dig deep into the lives and presidencies of Lincoln, Johnson, and the two Roosevelts. We'll trace their journeys from childhood to the White House, examining the experiences and influences that shaped them along the way.

For each president, we'll explore:

1. Their early years and formative experiences
2. Their entry into politics and rise to national prominence
3. Their presidencies, including key decisions, policies, and challenges
4. Their lasting impact on American politics and society

After exploring each presidency in detail, we'll step back and look at overarching themes and lessons. We'll examine how these presidents handled crisis management, approached issues of social justice, tackled economic challenges, and shaped America's role in the world.

Finally, we'll bring it all together, distilling key leadership principles and discussing how they can be applied to our current national challenges.

The goal is not just to inform, but to inspire and equip. By the end of this book, readers should have a deeper understanding of these four transformative presidencies, a clearer perspective on current political issues, and practical insights they can apply in their own lives and communities.

Part I: Abraham Lincoln - From Log Cabin to the White House (1861 - 1865)

1. Lincoln's Early Years

A Humble Beginning

On a cold winter's day in 1809, in a one-room log cabin on Sinking Spring Farm near Hodgenville, Kentucky, Abraham Lincoln entered the world. Born to Thomas Lincoln and Nancy Hanks Lincoln, young Abe's early life was far from the halls of power he would one day walk. The Lincoln family, like many others on the American frontier, lived a life of hardship and constant struggle.

The cabin where Lincoln was born was crude by today's standards - a single room with a dirt floor, no windows, and a stick-clay chimney. It's hard for us to imagine a future president starting life in such modest circumstances. Yet, these humble beginnings would shape Lincoln's character and inform his political views for years to come.

Lincoln's father, Thomas, was a farmer and carpenter who could barely read or write. His mother, Nancy, was literate and encouraged young Abe's curiosity and love for learning. This early exposure to the value of education, despite the family's limited means, planted seeds that would grow throughout Lincoln's life.

The Move to Indiana

When Abe was seven years old, the Lincoln family moved to Indiana. The reason? Land disputes in Kentucky had left Thomas Lincoln uncertain about his property rights. Indiana, newly admitted to the Union, offered more secure land titles under the Northwest Ordinance.

The journey to their new home was not an easy one. The family, along with their belongings, traveled by horse and wagon through dense forests and across rivers. Young Abe likely helped his father clear the path, an early taste of the physical labor that would define much of his youth.

Their new home in Indiana was, if anything, even more primitive than the one they left behind. The Lincolns initially lived in a "half-faced camp," a crude structure with three walls and an open front. It was in this harsh environment that young Abe began to develop the physical strength and resilience that would serve him well throughout his life.

Tragedy Strikes

Life on the frontier was hard, and tragedy was never far away. When Abe was just nine years old, his mother Nancy fell ill with "milk sickness," a disease caused by drinking milk from cows that had eaten poisonous plants. She died within a week, leaving young Abe devastated.

The loss of his mother was a profound blow to Lincoln. He later recalled, "All that I am, or hope to be, I owe to my angel mother." This early encounter with loss and grief likely contributed to the melancholy that would characterize Lincoln's personality throughout his life.

A year after Nancy's death, Thomas Lincoln married Sarah Bush Johnston, a widow with three children of her own. Sarah proved to be a kind and supportive stepmother who encouraged Abe's love of learning. She brought books into the household and supported Abe's efforts to educate himself, despite his father's skepticism about the value of book learning.

The School of Hard Work

Lincoln's childhood was dominated by hard physical labor. From a young age, he worked alongside his father, clearing land, planting crops, and splitting rails for fences. This work was backbreaking and constant, leaving little time for formal education.

In fact, Lincoln's formal schooling amounted to less than a year in total, spread out in bits and pieces as circumstances allowed. But Lincoln was determined to learn. He would walk miles to borrow books, and he read voraciously by firelight after long days of work.

This self-directed learning, pursued in the face of significant obstacles, speaks volumes about Lincoln's character. It shows a determination and thirst for knowledge that would serve him well throughout his life. It also gave him a deep appreciation for the value of education and self-improvement, themes that would resurface in his political career.

Shaping of Character

So, what influences shaped the character and values of the young Abraham Lincoln? Several key factors stand out:

1. The Frontier Experience: Growing up on the American frontier instilled in Lincoln a strong work ethic and a practical, problem-solving approach to life. It also gave him a firsthand understanding of the challenges faced by ordinary Americans, an understanding that would inform his political views and policies.

2. Family Dynamics: The loss of his mother at a young age, followed by the positive influence of his stepmother, likely contributed to Lincoln's emotional depth and his ability to handle adversity. His father's skepticism about book learning, contrasted with his stepmother's encouragement, may have fueled Lincoln's determination to educate himself.

3. Self-Directed Learning: Lincoln's pursuit of education, often in the face of significant obstacles, developed his intellectual curiosity and his belief in the power of self-improvement. This would later translate into his support for public education and land-grant colleges.

4. Physical Labor: The hard physical work of frontier life not only developed Lincoln's famous physical strength but also gave him a deep respect for labor and laborers. This would later influence his political and economic views, including his support for free labor over slave labor.

5. Exposure to Slavery: Although slavery was less prevalent in Indiana than in Kentucky, Lincoln's early exposure to the institution left a lasting impression. He later recalled seeing slaves chained together being transported down the Ohio River, an image that stayed with him and influenced his views on the issue.

6. Religious Influence: While Lincoln never joined a church, he was exposed to Baptist and Methodist preaching in his youth. This influenced his moral framework and his use of biblical language and imagery in his speeches and writings.

The Storyteller Emerges

One of Lincoln's most famous characteristics as an adult was his skill as a storyteller. This ability began to develop in his youth. In the evenings, after long days of work, Lincoln would entertain his family and neighbors with jokes, stories, and imitations. This wasn't just entertainment; it was a valuable skill in frontier society.

The ability to tell a good story or deliver a joke well could help ease tensions, build relationships, and communicate ideas effectively. Lincoln was honing a skill that would later serve him well in law and politics.

A Glimpse of the Future

Even in these early years, there were hints of the leader Lincoln would become. His stepmother later recalled, "Abe was the best boy I ever saw or ever expect to see." She noted his honesty, his kindness, and his eagerness to learn.

Lincoln's early experiences with public speaking came in an unusual form. He would often climb onto a stump in the fields and deliver impromptu "speeches" to his fellow workers, sometimes mimicking traveling preachers or politicians he had heard. Little did he know that he was practicing for a future in which his words would help shape a nation.

As Lincoln entered his late teens, he began to chafe at the limitations of frontier life. He wanted more than the life of a farmer. He took jobs working on ferryboats on the Ohio River, exposing him to a wider world and sparking his interest in law and politics. At the age of 21, Lincoln left his family's home to strike out on his own. He helped navigate a flatboat down the Mississippi to New Orleans, his first real journey into the wider world. This trip exposed him to the bustling commerce of the river and gave him his first real glimpse of urban life and the slave markets of the South.

The seeds of greatness were already present in the gangly, self-educated young man who set out from Indiana. The hardships of frontier life, the love of learning, the experience of loss, the physical strength gained from years of hard work, the moral framework shaped by his upbringing - all of these would play a role in shaping the man who would one day lead the nation through its greatest crisis.

2. Political Awakening

A New Chapter in New Salem

As the 1830s dawned, Abraham Lincoln found himself in New Salem, Illinois, a small frontier village that would become the stage for his political awakening. At 22 years old, Lincoln was still finding his footing in the world. Tall, gangly, and with little formal education, he might have seemed an unlikely candidate for future political stardom. Yet, it was here in New Salem that Lincoln began to develop the skills and reputation that would propel him into public life.

Lincoln took on various jobs in New Salem - clerk, postmaster, surveyor - each role expanding his network and honing his people skills. But it was his self-study of grammar and law that truly set the stage for his future career. Often, he could be found sprawled under a tree, poring over borrowed law books, determined to better himself through education.

The Spark of Political Ambition

In 1832, Lincoln made his first bid for public office, running for the Illinois General Assembly. Though he lost this initial race, his campaign speech showcased themes that would define his political career: support for education, infrastructure improvements, and economic opportunity. Even in defeat, Lincoln was laying the groundwork for future success.

Two years later, Lincoln tried again and won a seat in the state legislature. This victory marked the official start of his political career, but it was also a personal triumph. For a young man who had grown up in poverty with little formal education, election to the state legislature was a significant achievement.

During his time in the legislature, Lincoln allied himself with the Whig Party, advocating for internal improvements and economic development. He also took his first public stance against slavery, co-authoring a protest against pro-slavery resolutions in the Illinois legislature. This early stand, while cautious by later standards, hinted at the moral courage that would define his presidency.

From Politician to Lawyer

While serving in the legislature, Lincoln continued his legal studies. In 1836, he was admitted to the Illinois bar, opening a new chapter in his career. Lincoln's legal practice became the cornerstone of his professional life for the next two decades.

As a lawyer, Lincoln gained a reputation for honesty and sharp reasoning. He handled all sorts of cases, from petty disputes to murder trials. This wide-ranging practice exposed him to people from all walks of life and deepened his understanding of human nature.

One of Lincoln's most famous cases was his defense of William "Duff" Armstrong, accused of murder. Lincoln used an almanac to prove that the moon's position on the night of the crime made it impossible for the key witness to have seen what he claimed. This clever use of evidence showcased Lincoln's analytical skills and his ability to present complex ideas in simple, persuasive terms.

Lincoln's legal career wasn't just about winning cases; it was also about building relationships and honing his public speaking skills. Court appearances gave him ample opportunity to practice the art of persuasion, a skill that would serve him well in his political career.

The Prairie Lawyer Goes to Washington

In 1846, Lincoln's political ambitions took him to Washington D.C. as a member of the U.S. House of Representatives. His single term in Congress was relatively unremarkable, but it gave him valuable experience on the national stage.

Lincoln's most notable action in Congress was his opposition to the Mexican-American War. He introduced a series of resolutions, known as the "Spot Resolutions," challenging President Polk to prove that the war had started on American soil, as Polk claimed. This stance was unpopular with many of Lincoln's constituents and may have contributed to his decision not to seek re-election.

After his term in Congress, Lincoln returned to Illinois and his law practice. He thought his political career might be over, later writing that he was "losing interest in politics" and that his opposition to the Mexican-American War had likely left him "nearly politically dead."

The Kansas-Nebraska Act: A Political Reawakening

In 1854, a seismic shift in American politics reignited Lincoln's political passion. The Kansas-Nebraska Act, championed by Illinois Senator Stephen Douglas, allowed new states to decide for themselves whether to permit slavery. This effectively repealed the Missouri Compromise, which had prohibited slavery in much of the western territories.

Lincoln saw the Kansas-Nebraska Act as a dangerous expansion of slavery. In a series of speeches, he articulated his opposition to the spread of slavery into new territories. His most famous speech from this period, delivered in Peoria, Illinois, laid out his moral and practical arguments against slavery's expansion.

The Peoria speech marked Lincoln's re-emergence as a political force. He argued that the founders had put slavery on the path to eventual extinction, and that the Kansas-Nebraska Act threatened to breathe new life into the institution. Lincoln's eloquence and moral clarity in this speech catapulted him back into the political spotlight.

The Birth of the Republican Party

The political upheaval caused by the Kansas-Nebraska Act led to the formation of the Republican Party, a coalition of anti-slavery forces from various political backgrounds. Lincoln, with his clear stance against the expansion of slavery, found a natural home in this new party.

In 1856, at the Illinois Republican convention, Lincoln delivered another powerful speech against the spread of slavery. Known as the "Lost Speech" because no transcript survives, it reportedly electrified the audience and solidified Lincoln's position as a leading voice in the new party.

The Lincoln-Douglas Debates: A National Spotlight

In 1858, Lincoln challenged Stephen Douglas for his U.S. Senate seat. This campaign would produce one of the most famous series of political debates in American history: the Lincoln-Douglas debates.

The debates, seven in total, were held in towns across Illinois. They drew large crowds and received national press coverage. The central issue was slavery, particularly its potential expansion into new territories. Douglas argued for "popular sovereignty," allowing new states to decide the slavery question for themselves. Lincoln, in contrast, argued that slavery was a moral wrong and that its expansion should be halted.

One of Lincoln's most powerful moments came in the debate at Alton, where he said:

"That is the real issue. That is the issue that will continue in this country when these poor tongues of Judge Douglas and myself shall be silent. It is the eternal struggle between these two principles - right and wrong - throughout the world."

The debates showcased Lincoln's political and rhetorical skills. He had a talent for breaking down complex issues into simple, powerful statements. He used humor and folksy anecdotes to connect with his audience, while also demonstrating a deep understanding of constitutional law and political philosophy.

Although Lincoln lost the Senate race, the debates catapulted him to national prominence. His arguments against the expansion of slavery resonated with many in the North, and transcripts of the debates were widely circulated.

The Cooper Union Speech: A Presidential Contender Emerges

In February 1860, Lincoln delivered a speech at Cooper Union in New York City that would prove to be a turning point in his political career. In this address, Lincoln provided a scholarly analysis of the founders' views on federal power to regulate slavery in the territories.

The speech was a triumph. Lincoln demonstrated not just his moral opposition to slavery, but his intellectual grasp of constitutional history. The New York Tribune declared that "No man ever before made such an impression on his first appeal to a New York audience."

The Cooper Union speech established Lincoln as a serious contender for the Republican presidential nomination. It showed that this self-educated lawyer from Illinois could hold his own among the nation's political elite.

As the 1860 Republican National Convention approached, Lincoln was still considered an underdog for the nomination. Yet his political journey - from frontier poverty to national prominence - had prepared him for this moment. The skills he had honed as a lawyer, legislator, and debater would now be put to the ultimate test. The convention would be Lincoln's chance to secure the nomination and take the next step on his improbable path to the presidency. As he prepared for the convention, the nation stood on the brink of a crisis that would define his presidency and change the course of American history.

3. Presidency and the Civil War

A Nation Divided

On March 4, 1861, Abraham Lincoln stood on the steps of the U.S. Capitol to take the oath of office as the 16th President of the United States. The atmosphere was tense. Seven Southern states had already seceded from the Union, and more would soon follow. As Lincoln raised his hand to swear the oath, he faced a nation on the brink of civil war.

In his inaugural address, Lincoln attempted to reassure the South that he had no intention of interfering with slavery where it already existed. He appealed to the "better angels of our nature," urging Americans to remember the bonds that united them. But his words fell on deaf ears in the South, where many viewed his election as a threat to their way of life.

The new president faced a daunting task. He had to preserve the Union, but how? Could war be avoided? And if not, how could the nation survive such a conflict?

The Storm Breaks

Lincoln's hopes for a peaceful resolution were dashed on April 12, 1861, when Confederate forces fired on Fort Sumter in Charleston harbor. The Civil War had begun.

The early days of the war were chaotic. Lincoln, who had no military experience, found himself thrust into the role of Commander-in-Chief. He spent long hours poring over military maps and telegraph reports, trying to grasp the strategies and tactics of warfare.

One of Lincoln's first challenges was to rally the North behind the war effort. In a special session of Congress on July 4, 1861, he argued that the conflict was about more than just the Union – it was a test of democracy itself. "This is essentially a people's contest," he declared, framing the war as a struggle to prove that democratic government could survive in a time of crisis.

Lincoln's leadership style during the war was marked by a combination of firmness and flexibility. He was willing to listen to diverse opinions and change course when necessary, but he never wavered from his core goal of preserving the Union.

The Search for a General

One of Lincoln's most frustrating challenges was finding effective military leadership. He cycled through a series of commanding generals, each of whom disappointed him in different ways.

George McClellan, for instance, was a brilliant organizer who turned the Union Army into a formidable fighting force. But he was overly cautious, reluctant to engage the enemy even when he had superior numbers. Lincoln's frustration with McClellan's inaction led to one of his famous quips. When told that McClellan was suffering from "the slows," Lincoln replied, "Yes, he's got the slows. Has had them all his life."

Lincoln's search for an effective general was not just a military matter – it had significant political implications as well. Each setback on the battlefield emboldened critics of the war and threatened to erode public support for the Union cause.

It wasn't until later in the war, with the emergence of generals like Ulysses S. Grant and William Tecumseh Sherman, that Lincoln found the aggressive, determined military leadership he had been seeking.

A New Birth of Freedom

As the war dragged on, Lincoln began to see that the conflict offered an opportunity to address the issue of slavery directly. He had always opposed slavery on moral grounds, but as president, he had been cautious about taking action against the institution, fearing it would drive border states into the Confederacy.

By the summer of 1862, however, Lincoln had concluded that emancipation could serve both moral and military purposes. Freeing the slaves in rebel states would deprive the Confederacy of a significant labor force and potentially provide new recruits for the Union Army.

On September 22, 1862, following the Union victory at Antietam, Lincoln issued the Preliminary Emancipation Proclamation. This document gave the Confederate states 100 days to return to the Union or have their slaves declared free.

The Emancipation Proclamation

On January 1, 1863, with no Confederate states having returned to the Union, Lincoln signed the Emancipation Proclamation. This historic document declared "that all persons held as slaves" within the rebellious states "are, and henceforward shall be free." The immediate practical effects of the Proclamation were limited. It applied only to areas under Confederate control, exempting slave-holding border states and already-occupied parts of the Confederacy. Critics pointed out that it freed slaves precisely where the federal government had no power to do so.

But the symbolic impact of the Emancipation Proclamation was enormous. It transformed the nature of the conflict, making the abolition of slavery an explicit war aim of the Union. As Lincoln himself put it, "I never, in my life, felt more certain that I was doing right, than I do in signing this paper."

The Proclamation also had significant diplomatic effects. By framing the war as a struggle against slavery, Lincoln made it much more difficult for European powers, particularly Britain and France, to intervene on behalf of the Confederacy.

Moreover, the Proclamation opened the door for African Americans to join the Union Army in large numbers. By the end of the war, nearly 200,000 Black soldiers and sailors had served in Union forces, playing a crucial role in the eventual Northern victory.

The Gettysburg Address

In November 1863, Lincoln traveled to Gettysburg, Pennsylvania, to dedicate a national cemetery on the site of the bloodiest battle of the war. His speech that day, now known as the Gettysburg Address, would become one of the most famous in American history.

In just 272 words, Lincoln reframed the entire meaning of the war and, indeed, of American democracy itself. He began by reaching back to the nation's founding: "Four score and seven years ago, our fathers brought forth on this continent a new nation, conceived in liberty, and dedicated to the proposition that all men are created equal."

Lincoln then connected the sacrifices of the soldiers at Gettysburg to the ongoing struggle to realize the promise of American democracy. The war, he said, was a test of whether "that nation, or any nation so conceived, and so dedicated, can long endure."

Finally, Lincoln looked to the future, calling on the living to rededicate themselves to the unfinished work of those who had died. The great task remaining, he said, was to ensure "that government of the people, by the people, for the people, shall not perish from the earth."

The Gettysburg Address solidified the connection between the Union cause and the broader ideals of human freedom and equality. It remains a powerful articulation of the principles underlying American democracy.

The Tide Turns

As the war entered its later stages, the tide began to turn in favor of the Union. The victory at Gettysburg in July 1863, coupled with the fall of Vicksburg, Mississippi, marked a turning point in the conflict. Lincoln finally found the aggressive generalship he had been seeking in Ulysses S. Grant. Unlike previous Union commanders, Grant was willing to use the North's superior numbers and resources to wear down the Confederate armies.

Lincoln's relationship with Grant was one of mutual trust and respect. When critics complained about Grant's heavy casualties and alleged drinking habits, Lincoln replied, "I can't spare this man. He fights."

As military victory began to seem more certain, Lincoln turned his attention to the challenge of reuniting the nation. His policy of reconciliation was summed up in his Second Inaugural Address, delivered on March 4, 1865. In this speech, remarkable for its lack of triumphalism, Lincoln called for healing "with malice toward none, with charity for all."

The Last Full Measure of Devotion

Just over a month after his Second Inaugural, with the war all but won, Lincoln's life was cut short by an assassin's bullet. On April 14, 1865, while attending a play at Ford's Theatre in Washington, he was shot by John Wilkes Booth, a Confederate sympathizer. Lincoln died the next morning.

The nation was plunged into mourning. Even many who had opposed Lincoln in life now recognized the magnitude of his achievements. He had preserved the Union, ended slavery, and articulated a vision of democracy that continues to inspire people around the world.

Lincoln's death left the enormous task of Reconstruction to his successor, Andrew Johnson. The challenges of reuniting the nation and securing the rights of freed slaves would prove to be as daunting as the war itself.

Reflecting on Lincoln's presidency, we see a leader who grew in office, rising to meet unprecedented challenges. He combined political shrewdness with moral conviction, pragmatism with idealism. His words and actions continue to shape our understanding of democracy, equality, and national unity.

The legacy of Lincoln's leadership during the Civil War extends far beyond his own time. His commitment to preserving the Union at all costs, his evolution on the issue of slavery, and his vision of a "new birth of freedom" continue to resonate in American politics and society.

4. Lincoln's Leadership Legacy

A Presidency That Shaped a Nation

Abraham Lincoln's presidency was a watershed moment in American history. His leadership during the Civil War not only preserved the Union but also fundamentally altered the course of American democracy. More than 150 years after his death, Lincoln's impact on the presidency and American political life remains profound.

Expanding Presidential Power

One of Lincoln's most significant legacies was his expansion of presidential power. Faced with a national crisis of unprecedented scale, Lincoln took actions that pushed the boundaries of executive authority. He suspended the writ of habeas corpus, imposed a naval blockade on Southern ports, and authorized military spending without Congressional approval. These actions were controversial at the time and remain subjects of debate among historians and legal scholars. Critics argued that Lincoln had overstepped his constitutional authority. Lincoln, however, maintained that the president's oath to "preserve, protect and defend the Constitution" gave him extraordinary powers in times of rebellion or invasion.

Lincoln's expansive view of presidential power set a precedent that future presidents would invoke in times of crisis. From Franklin D. Roosevelt during the Great Depression and World War II to George W. Bush after the 9/11 attacks, presidents have cited Lincoln's example to justify broad executive actions.

Redefining American Democracy

Perhaps Lincoln's greatest legacy was his redefinition of American democracy. In the Gettysburg Address, Lincoln articulated a vision of "government of the people, by the people, for the people" that continues to inspire democratic movements worldwide.

Lincoln's presidency marked a shift in how Americans understood their relationship to the federal government. Before the Civil War, many Americans' primary loyalty was to their state rather than the nation. Lincoln's insistence on preserving the Union helped cement the idea of a united American nation.

Moreover, Lincoln's support for the 13th Amendment, which abolished slavery, began the long process of expanding the definition of American citizenship. Though full equality was still far off, Lincoln's actions set the stage for the civil rights movements of the future.

The Power of Words

Lincoln's mastery of language and his ability to communicate complex ideas in simple, powerful terms set a new standard for presidential rhetoric. His speeches, from the Gettysburg Address to his Second Inaugural, are studied not just for their historical significance but for their literary merit.

Lincoln understood the power of words to inspire, console, and persuade. He used stories and analogies to make his points, often leveling serious discussions with humor. This approach made his ideas accessible to a wide audience and helped him build public support for his policies.

Future presidents would follow Lincoln's example, recognizing the importance of effective communication in leadership. Franklin D. Roosevelt's fireside chats, John F. Kennedy's inaugural address, and Ronald Reagan's speeches all echo Lincoln's ability to connect with the American people through powerful, plainspoken rhetoric.

Leadership Qualities for Today

As we examine Lincoln's legacy, several leadership qualities stand out as particularly relevant for today's leaders, whether in politics, business, or community service.

1. Moral Courage

Lincoln's stance against slavery, even when it was politically risky, exemplifies moral courage. He was willing to take unpopular positions when he believed they were right. In our own time, when leaders often seem guided more by polls than principles, Lincoln's moral courage serves as a powerful example.

Consider how this quality might apply in your own life or work. Have you ever had to stand up for what you believed was right, even when it wasn't popular? Lincoln's example reminds us that true leadership often requires the courage to challenge the status quo.

2. Adaptability and Growth

Lincoln's presidency was marked by continuous learning and adaptation. He entered office with little executive or military experience, but he worked tirelessly to educate himself on the issues he faced. He was willing to change his strategies when they weren't working and to listen to diverse viewpoints. In today's rapidly changing world, the ability to adapt and grow is more important than ever. Lincoln's example encourages us to remain open to new ideas and to view challenges as opportunities for learning and growth.

3. Emotional Intelligence

Despite his melancholic tendencies, Lincoln displayed remarkable emotional intelligence. He was able to manage his own emotions under extreme stress and showed empathy towards others, even his political opponents. His ability to build and maintain relationships was key to his political success.

In our increasingly interconnected world, emotional intelligence is a critical leadership skill. Lincoln's example reminds us of the importance of understanding and managing both our own emotions and those of others.

4. Resilience in Times of Adversity

Lincoln's life and presidency were marked by numerous setbacks and tragedies, from his humble beginnings to military defeats to personal losses. Yet he persevered, maintaining his commitment to his goals even in the darkest hours of the Civil War. Resilience - the ability to bounce back from setbacks - is a vital quality for leaders in any field. Lincoln's life teaches us that failure is not final, and that persistence in a time of adversity can lead to remarkable achievements.

5. Visionary Thinking

While dealing with the immediate crises of the Civil War, Lincoln never lost sight of the larger issues at stake. He saw the conflict not just as a struggle to preserve the Union, but as a test of whether democracy itself could survive. This ability to connect day-to-day actions with long-term goals is a hallmark of visionary leadership.

In our own lives and work, we can strive to emulate Lincoln's ability to see the bigger picture. How do our daily actions contribute to our long-term goals? How can we inspire others with a vision of a better future?

6. Humility and Self-Awareness

Despite his remarkable achievements, Lincoln maintained a sense of humility throughout his life. He was aware of his own limitations and was not afraid to surround himself with people who could complement his skills - even former rivals, as evidenced by his "Team of Rivals" cabinet.

In an age often characterized by self-promotion and ego, Lincoln's humility is refreshing and instructive. It reminds us that true leadership is not about personal glory, but about achieving results and empowering others.

Applying Lincoln's Legacy Today

As we face our own national challenges - political polarization, economic inequality, racial tensions - Lincoln's leadership offers valuable lessons.

Like Lincoln, we must be willing to confront difficult issues head-on, even when doing so is politically risky. We must strive to communicate in ways that unite rather than divide, appealing to our shared values and common humanity.

We can learn from Lincoln's ability to balance idealism with pragmatism. While never losing sight of his ultimate goals, Lincoln was willing to compromise and make incremental progress when necessary. This approach - holding firm to core principles while remaining flexible on details - can be invaluable in handling complex political and social issues.

Lincoln's example also teaches us about the importance of personal growth and lifelong learning. In a world of rapid technological and social change, leaders must continually adapt and acquire new skills. Lincoln's transformation from a frontier lawyer to a wartime president reminds us that leadership is a journey of continuous improvement.

Perhaps most importantly, Lincoln's legacy challenges us to think deeply about the meaning of democracy and the responsibilities of citizenship. As citizens, we can honor Lincoln's legacy by engaging actively in the democratic process, standing up for our principles, and working to bridge the divides in our society. We can strive to emulate his commitment to equality and his belief in the dignity of all people.

Lincoln's leadership during America's greatest crisis set a standard against which all future presidents would be measured. But his legacy is not just for presidents or political leaders. It offers lessons for all of us as we face our own challenges and strive to make a positive impact in our communities and our world.

Part II: Theodore Roosevelt - The Energetic Reformer (1901 - 1909)

1. Roosevelt's Childhood and Youth

A Sickly Start

On October 27, 1858, in a brownstone at 28 East 20th Street in New York City, Theodore Roosevelt Jr. entered the world. Born into a wealthy family, young "Teedie," as he was nicknamed, seemed destined for a life of privilege. However, his early years were far from easy.

From infancy, Roosevelt struggled with debilitating asthma attacks that often left him gasping for air. These episodes were so severe that the family feared for his life. In an era before effective treatments for asthma, the Roosevelts tried everything from coffee to cigar smoke to ease Teedie's breathing. The image of the young Roosevelt - frail, bespectacled, and struggling to breathe - stands in stark contrast to the robust, energetic man he would become. His childhood illness shaped his character in profound ways, instilling in him a determination to overcome physical limitations that would define his approach to life.

Despite his physical challenges, Roosevelt was a curious and energetic child. He developed an early passion for natural history, spending hours observing and cataloging the wildlife around him. This interest would stay with him throughout his life, influencing his later conservation efforts as president.

A Family of Influence

The Roosevelt family played a crucial role in shaping Theodore's character and ambitions. His father, Theodore Roosevelt Sr., was a prominent businessman and philanthropist. Known as "Thee" to his family, he set a powerful example of civic responsibility and moral uprightness for his children.

Young Teedie idolized his father, later writing, "My father, Theodore Roosevelt, was the best man I ever knew. He combined strength and courage with gentleness, tenderness, and great unselfishness." The elder Roosevelt's emphasis on moral character and public service left an indelible mark on his son. Roosevelt's mother, Martha "Mittie" Bulloch Roosevelt, came from a prominent Southern family. She brought a love of literature and storytelling to the Roosevelt household, nurturing Theodore's intellectual curiosity and imagination.

The contrast between his Northern father and Southern mother exposed young Theodore to different perspectives from an early age. This family dynamic, set against the backdrop of the Civil War, gave Roosevelt a nuanced understanding of the nation's divisions and a desire to bridge them.

Roosevelt's siblings also played important roles in his development. His older sister Anna, known as "Bamie," was a source of support and guidance throughout his life. His younger brother Elliott (who would later become the father of Eleanor Roosevelt) and sister Corinne were his playmates and confidants.

Overcoming Adversity

As a child, Roosevelt was told by a doctor that due to his weak heart, he should avoid strenuous activity. Instead of accepting this limitation, Roosevelt, with his father's encouragement, embarked on a rigorous program of physical activity to strengthen his body. He took up boxing, weightlifting, and horseback riding. He hiked, swam, and climbed. This self-improvement regimen became a lifelong habit, shaping Roosevelt's belief in the value of "the strenuous life" and his conviction that individuals could overcome almost any obstacle through sheer willpower and effort.

Roosevelt's struggle with illness also fostered in him a deep empathy for those facing physical challenges. This compassion would later influence his political views, particularly his support for public health initiatives and workplace safety regulations.

The Power of Education

Education played a central role in Roosevelt's youth. Due to his frequent illnesses, much of his early education took place at home under the guidance of tutors and his parents. This unconventional schooling allowed Roosevelt to pursue his interests in natural history and literature with a freedom that would have been impossible in a traditional classroom.

Roosevelt devoured books on a wide range of subjects, developing the broad knowledge base that would later make him one of the most intellectually curious presidents in American history. His passion for reading and learning stayed with him throughout his life, shaping his approach to politics and governance.

When Roosevelt did attend formal schooling, he excelled academically. He entered Harvard College in 1876, where he continued to pursue his interests in natural history and began to develop his skills as a writer and orator.

The Making of a Leader

Even in his youth, Roosevelt displayed many of the qualities that would define his later leadership. His boundless energy, his intellectual curiosity, his moral certainty, and his determination to overcome obstacles were all evident from an early age.

Roosevelt's childhood experiences taught him valuable lessons about perseverance, self-improvement, and the importance of moral character. These lessons would shape his approach to politics and inform his vision for the nation.

The transformation of the sickly child into the vigorous young man became a central part of Roosevelt's personal mythology. It reinforced his belief in the power of willpower and self-discipline, themes that would recur throughout his political career.

European Adventures and Personal Growth

In 1869 and 1870, the Roosevelt family embarked on a grand tour of Europe. This experience broadened young Theodore's horizons, exposing him to different cultures and histories. It fueled his interest in international affairs and gave him a global perspective that would later influence his foreign policy as president.

During this trip, Roosevelt had a transformative experience in Egypt. While on a Nile cruise, he saw two dead Nubian boys who had been killed by an Englishman. The incident left a deep impression on Roosevelt, reinforcing his belief in the importance of justice and the rule of law.

The loss of the first Theodore Roosevelt in 1878 was a profound shock to young Theodore. He idolized his father, and the loss spurred him to live up to the example of moral rectitude and public service that his father had set. Roosevelt would later write, "I have tried to live up to his principles and act as he would have acted."

Following his father's death, Roosevelt threw himself into his studies at Harvard with renewed vigor. He also began to take a more active interest in politics, laying the groundwork for his future career.

The Foundations of a Political Philosophy

As Roosevelt entered adulthood, the experiences and influences of his youth coalesced into a distinct political philosophy. His belief in the power of individual effort, his sense of moral certainty, his fascination with nature and conservation, his commitment to public service, and his conviction that the strong had a duty to protect the weak - all these elements can be traced back to his formative years.

Roosevelt's childhood and youth set the stage for the leader he would become. The sickly boy who refused to be limited by his physical weakness grew into a man determined to push himself and his nation to greatness. The curious child who loved nature became a president who would champion conservation. The young man shaped by strong family values became a political leader with a deep sense of moral purpose.

2. Early Political Career

The Young Reformer in Albany

Theodore Roosevelt's entry into politics came early. In 1881, at the age of 23, he was elected to the New York State Assembly. This marked the beginning of a political career that would eventually lead him to the White House.

From the moment he arrived in Albany, Roosevelt made waves. His youth, energy, and reformist zeal set him apart from the older, more conservative politicians who dominated the legislature. Roosevelt quickly gained a reputation as a fighter against corruption and a champion of good government.

During his time in the Assembly, Roosevelt tackled a range of issues. He pushed for civil service reform, aiming to replace the corrupt spoils system with a merit-based approach to government appointments. He also advocated for better working conditions and fought against corporate influence in politics.

One of Roosevelt's most notable achievements in the Assembly was his investigation into the New York City government. His efforts exposed corruption in the city's court system and led to the impeachment of a Supreme Court Justice. This investigation established Roosevelt as a fearless reformer and gained him national attention.

Roosevelt's time in the Assembly was not without challenges. He faced opposition from entrenched political interests and was often criticized for his brash style and unwillingness to compromise. Yet, these early political battles honed his skills as a legislator and public speaker, preparing him for the larger stages to come.

The Cowboy Interlude

Roosevelt's political career took an unexpected turn in 1884. Devastated by the deaths of his wife and mother on the same day, he retreated to the Dakota Territory, where he spent two years as a cattle rancher. This period, while a departure from politics, proved formative for Roosevelt's character and his understanding of the American West.

His experiences in the West deepened his appreciation for nature and conservation, themes that would feature prominently in his later political career. It also reinforced his belief in the value of "the strenuous life" and his admiration for the rugged individualism of the frontier.

Back to the Political Arena

Returning to New York in 1886, Roosevelt re-entered politics with renewed vigor. He ran for mayor of New York City but lost. Undeterred, he continued to build his political career, serving in various appointed positions.

In 1895, Roosevelt became President of the New York City Police Board. In this role, he applied his reformist zeal to the city's notoriously corrupt police department. He implemented a merit-based promotion system, cracked down on police corruption, and enforced laws that had long been ignored, including Sunday liquor laws.

Roosevelt's tenure as Police Commissioner was marked by both successes and controversies. His midnight walks to check on officers' performance became legendary, as did his efforts to modernize the department. However, his strict enforcement of unpopular laws, particularly the Sunday closing laws, drew criticism from some quarters.

Despite the challenges, Roosevelt's time as Police Commissioner further burnished his reputation as an energetic reformer unafraid to take on entrenched interests. It also gave him valuable executive experience that would serve him well in future roles.

Assistant Secretary of the Navy

In 1897, newly elected President William McKinley appointed Roosevelt as Assistant Secretary of the Navy. This position placed Roosevelt at the center of national politics and gave him a platform to advocate for his views on America's role in the world.

Roosevelt brought his characteristic energy and ambition to the job. He pushed for naval expansion and modernization, arguing that a strong navy was essential for America's security and global influence. He also advocated for the acquisition of overseas territories, seeing them as necessary for America's growing power and prestige.

During his time in this role, Roosevelt played a key part in preparing the Navy for the looming conflict with Spain. He ordered commodore George Dewey to move his squadron to Hong

Kong, positioning it to strike at the Spanish fleet in the Philippines when war broke out.

Roosevelt's expansionist views and his eagerness for military action sometimes put him at odds with his superiors, including Secretary of the Navy John Long. Yet, his foresight and preparations proved valuable when the Spanish-American War began in 1898.

The Rough Rider

When war with Spain erupted, Roosevelt saw an opportunity for adventure and glory. He resigned his position as Assistant Secretary of the Navy and, with the help of his friend Leonard Wood, organized a volunteer cavalry regiment known as the Rough Riders. The Rough Riders were a diverse group, including cowboys, Native Americans, and Ivy League athletes. Roosevelt's leadership and the unit's colorful composition captured the public's imagination, making them one of the most famous units of the war.

In Cuba, Roosevelt led his men in the famous charge up San Juan Hill. This action, while perhaps embellished in later retellings, cemented Roosevelt's reputation for bravery and leadership. It also provided him with a powerful personal narrative that would serve him well in his future political career.

Roosevelt returned from Cuba a war hero, his exploits splashed across newspaper headlines. This fame catapulted him into the national spotlight and set the stage for his rapid rise to the governorship of New York and, ultimately, the vice presidency and presidency.

Lessons in Leadership

Roosevelt's early political career offers several valuable lessons in leadership:

1. The Power of Reform: Roosevelt's commitment to reform and good government resonated with the public and set him apart from traditional politicians. His willingness to take on corruption and entrenched interests established him as a principled leader.

2. The Importance of Action: Throughout his career, Roosevelt emphasized action over words. Whether walking the streets of New York as Police Commissioner or leading charges in Cuba, he led by example.

3. The Value of Diverse Experiences: Roosevelt's varied experiences - from the New York Assembly to the Dakota Territory to the Navy Department - gave him a broad perspective that informed his later leadership.

4. The Role of Character: Roosevelt's personal qualities - his energy, his courage, his intellectual curiosity - were as important to his success as his policies. His larger-than-life personality helped him connect with the public and inspire followers.

5. The Power of Narrative: Roosevelt understood the importance of storytelling in politics. His experiences, particularly his military service, provided him with compelling personal narratives that resonated with the public.

Shaping a Political Philosophy

As Roosevelt moved through these early stages of his political career, his political philosophy began to take shape. He emerged as a progressive Republican, advocating for reform and a more active role for government in addressing social and economic issues.

His experiences in the Assembly and as Police Commissioner reinforced his belief in the need to curb corporate power and clean up government corruption. His time in the West gave him a deep appreciation for conservation and the need to protect America's natural resources.

Roosevelt's naval service and his experiences in the Spanish-American War solidified his belief in American exceptionalism and the country's role as a world power. These views would later inform his foreign policy as president.

Throughout these years, Roosevelt maintained his commitment to "the strenuous life" - the idea that individuals and nations grow stronger through challenge and effort. This philosophy underpinned both his personal conduct and his vision for the nation. As Roosevelt's star rose in national politics, he brought with him this combination of progressive domestic policies and assertive foreign policy. These ideas, along with his forceful personality and reform-minded approach, would define his presidency and leave a lasting impact on American politics.

Roosevelt's early career demonstrates how varied experiences can shape a leader's worldview and approach to governance. It shows the importance of principles and character in building a political base. And it illustrates how personal narrative can be a powerful tool in connecting with the public.

As we follow Roosevelt's journey to the presidency, we'll see how the lessons he learned and the reputation he built in these early years informed his actions on the national stage. The young reformer from New York, the cowboy from Dakota, and the Rough Rider from Cuba would all play a part in shaping the president Theodore Roosevelt would become.

3. Unexpected Presidency and Square Deal

An Assassin's Bullet Changes History

On September 6, 1901, President William McKinley was shot by anarchist Leon Czolgosz at the Pan-American Exposition in Buffalo, New York. Vice President Theodore Roosevelt rushed to Buffalo, but upon learning that McKinley's condition was improving, he left to join his family on a camping trip in the Adirondacks.

Days later, while hiking on Mount Marcy, Roosevelt received the news that McKinley's condition had worsened. He raced back to Buffalo, but McKinley died before he arrived. On September 14, 1901, in a small private ceremony, Theodore Roosevelt took the oath of office as the 26th President of the United States.

At 42, Roosevelt became the youngest president in the nation's history. His ascension to the presidency was unexpected and, for some, unwelcome. Conservative Republicans, wary of Roosevelt's reformist tendencies, had pushed for his nomination as Vice

President precisely to sideline him. Now, this energetic and unpredictable man was suddenly at the helm of the nation.

Roosevelt wasted no time in making his mark. In his first address to Congress, he laid out an ambitious domestic agenda that would come to be known as the "Square Deal." This program aimed to balance the interests of business, consumers, and workers while also protecting the nation's natural resources.

The Square Deal: A New Vision for America

Roosevelt's Square Deal was built on three main ideas: conservation of natural resources, control of corporations, and consumer protection. These principles reflected Roosevelt's belief that the government had a responsibility to act as a fair arbiter between competing interests in society.

The name "Square Deal" itself was significant. It conveyed Roosevelt's commitment to fairness and his belief that all Americans, regardless of their social or economic status, deserved an equal chance to succeed. This idea resonated with many Americans who felt that the rapid industrialization of the late 19th century had created an uneven playing field.

Roosevelt's approach represented a departure from the laissez-faire policies of previous administrations. He believed that the federal government should take an active role in regulating the economy and addressing social issues. This philosophy, which came to be known as "New Nationalism," would have a lasting impact on American politics.

Trust-Busting: Taking on Big Business

One of the most significant aspects of Roosevelt's Square Deal was his approach to big business. The late 19th and early 20th centuries had seen the rise of powerful corporations, often referred to as "trusts," that dominated entire industries. Many Americans felt these trusts had become too powerful and were stifling competition and exploiting workers and consumers.

Roosevelt didn't oppose big business on principle. He recognized the economic benefits that large corporations could bring. However, he believed that when companies abused their power or acted against the public interest, the government had a duty to step in.

In 1902, Roosevelt made his first major move against the trusts by challenging the Northern Securities Company, a railroad monopoly. The Justice Department filed a lawsuit under the Sherman Antitrust Act, arguing that the company was an illegal monopoly. The case went all the way to the Supreme Court, which ruled in the government's favor in 1904.

This victory emboldened Roosevelt to take on other trusts. During his presidency, his administration initiated over 40 antitrust suits against major corporations, including Standard Oil and the American Tobacco Company. This earned Roosevelt the nickname "the trust-buster," although he preferred to think of himself as a "trust regulator."

Roosevelt's approach to trusts was more nuanced than simple opposition. He distinguished between "good" trusts that operated in the public interest and "bad" trusts that abused their power. His goal was not to destroy big business but to ensure it operated within the bounds of the law and for the benefit of the public.

Conservation: Protecting America's Natural Heritage

Another key component of Roosevelt's Square Deal was conservation. An avid outdoorsman and naturalist, Roosevelt was deeply concerned about the rapid depletion of America's natural resources. He believed that the government had a responsibility to protect these resources for future generations. During his presidency, Roosevelt dramatically expanded the nation's system of national parks, forests, and wildlife refuges. He established five new national parks, created the first 18 national monuments, and set aside over 230 million acres of public land for conservation.

Roosevelt's conservation efforts weren't just about preserving scenic beauty. He saw conservation as a matter of national importance, essential for the long-term economic and social well-being of the country. He argued that natural resources should be used wisely and sustainably, not exploited for short-term gain.

One of Roosevelt's most significant conservation achievements was the passage of the Newlands Reclamation Act in 1902. This law funded irrigation projects in the arid Western states, opening up new areas for agriculture and settlement. It reflected Roosevelt's belief that conservation and development could go hand in hand when managed properly.

Roosevelt also used his executive powers to advance conservation. In 1906, he signed the Antiquities Act, which gave the president the authority to designate national monuments. He used this power extensively, protecting areas like the Grand Canyon and Devil's Tower.

Consumer Protection: Safeguarding Public Health

The third pillar of Roosevelt's Square Deal focused on consumer protection. The rapid industrialization of the late 19th century had led to concerns about food safety and public health. Roosevelt believed the government had a responsibility to protect consumers from dangerous products and misleading advertising.

One of the most significant achievements in this area was the passage of the Pure Food and Drug Act and the Meat Inspection Act in 1906. These laws were prompted in part by Upton Sinclair's novel "The Jungle," which exposed unsanitary conditions in Chicago's meatpacking industry.

The Pure Food and Drug Act prohibited the sale of misbranded or adulterated food and drugs in interstate commerce. It also required that active ingredients be placed on the labels of drug products. The Meat Inspection Act mandated sanitary conditions in meatpacking plants and established a system of federal inspectors.

These laws marked a significant expansion of federal regulatory power and laid the groundwork for future consumer protection legislation. They reflected Roosevelt's belief that the government had a duty to protect public health and safety, even if it meant increased regulation of business.

Labor Relations: Seeking a Balance

While not typically listed as one of the main components of the Square Deal, Roosevelt's approach to labor relations was an important part of his domestic policy. He sought to balance the interests of workers and management, often intervening in labor disputes to seek fair resolutions.

One of Roosevelt's most famous interventions came during the Coal Strike of 1902. When coal mine owners refused to negotiate with striking workers, threatening a national fuel shortage, Roosevelt stepped in. He threatened to use federal troops to seize the mines if the owners didn't agree to arbitration. This bold move led to a settlement and burnished Roosevelt's reputation as a fair dealer.

Roosevelt's approach to labor issues was pragmatic rather than ideological. He supported some union demands, like the eight-hour workday for federal employees, but also used injunctions to halt strikes when he felt they threatened the public interest. His goal was to maintain industrial peace and ensure fair treatment for workers without undermining the fundamentals of the capitalist system.

The Legacy of the Square Deal

Roosevelt's Square Deal policies had a lasting impact on American politics and society. They expanded the role of the federal government in regulating the economy and protecting public welfare. This set the stage for later progressive reforms and influenced the development of the modern regulatory state.

The Square Deal also helped to redefine the Republican Party. Under Roosevelt, the party began to move away from its traditional pro-business stance towards a more progressive position. This shift would continue under Roosevelt's successors and would eventually lead to a realignment of American political parties.

Perhaps most importantly, the Square Deal established the principle that the government had a responsibility to act as a counterweight to powerful private interests. This idea would influence American political thought for generations to come, shaping debates about the proper role of government in society.

Roosevelt's presidency demonstrated how a leader with a clear vision and the will to act could use the power of the office to drive significant change. His energetic approach to governance, his willingness to take on powerful interests, and his ability to communicate his ideas to the public set a new standard for presidential leadership.

4. Roosevelt's Influence on Progressive Politics

Reshaping the Role of Government

Theodore Roosevelt's presidency marked a turning point in American political history. His vision of an active federal government, willing to intervene in economic and social affairs, represented a significant departure from the laissez-faire approach of the 19th century. Roosevelt believed that the government should act as a fair arbiter between competing interests in society, a concept he called the "Square Deal."

This shift in thinking about the role of government had far-reaching consequences. Roosevelt expanded federal power in ways that would have been unthinkable just a few decades earlier. He used the presidency as a "bully pulpit" to advocate for progressive reforms, arguing that the government had a responsibility to protect the public interest against powerful private entities. Roosevelt's approach to governance was rooted in his belief that the challenges of the 20th century required new solutions. The rapid industrialization and urbanization of the late 19th century had created social and economic problems that, in Roosevelt's view, could only be addressed through government action. This philosophy laid the groundwork for the modern regulatory state.

One of Roosevelt's most significant contributions was his expansion of presidential power. He took an expansive view of executive authority, arguing that the president could do anything not explicitly forbidden by the Constitution or laws. This interpretation of presidential power would influence future presidents and shape debates about executive authority for generations to come.

The Birth of Modern Environmentalism

Roosevelt's conservation efforts represent one of his most enduring legacies. His passion for nature and his belief in the government's role in protecting natural resources fundamentally altered America's approach to the environment.

During his presidency, Roosevelt set aside more than 230 million acres of public land for conservation. He established five national parks, 18 national monuments, 51 federal bird reservations, and

150 national forests. This massive expansion of protected lands laid the foundation for the modern environmental movement.

Roosevelt's conservation philosophy went beyond mere preservation. He advocated for the wise use of natural resources, balancing conservation with development. This approach, which he called "utilitarian conservation," sought to manage resources for the long-term benefit of the nation.

The impact of Roosevelt's conservation efforts continues to be felt today. The national parks and forests he established remain vital parts of America's natural heritage. His ideas about resource management and the government's role in conservation continue to inform environmental policy debates.

Regulating Big Business

Roosevelt's approach to business regulation represented another significant shift in the role of government. While he wasn't opposed to big business per se, Roosevelt believed that corporations should operate in the public interest. When they failed to do so, he argued, it was the government's duty to intervene. His "trust-busting" efforts set important legal precedents for antitrust enforcement. The successful prosecution of the Northern Securities

Company under the Sherman Antitrust Act demonstrated that the government could effectively challenge corporate monopolies. This set the stage for future antitrust actions and helped shape American economic policy.

Roosevelt's distinction between "good" trusts and "bad" trusts introduced a nuanced approach to business regulation. Rather than seeking to break up all large corporations, he aimed to ensure they operated fairly and in the public interest. This philosophy continues to influence discussions about corporate regulation and responsibility.

The Legacy of the Square Deal

The principles of Roosevelt's Square Deal - conservation of natural resources, control of corporations, and consumer protection - have had a lasting impact on American politics. These ideas formed the basis for many progressive reforms of the 20th century and continue to shape policy debates today.

Consumer protection laws, for instance, have their roots in Roosevelt-era legislation like the Pure Food and Drug Act. The idea that the government has a responsibility to protect consumers from dangerous products and fraudulent practices remains a cornerstone of American regulatory policy.

Similarly, Roosevelt's efforts to balance the interests of labor and management set important precedents. His willingness to intervene in labor disputes, as he did in the 1902 coal strike, established the federal government as a potential mediator in industrial conflicts. This role would expand significantly in subsequent decades.

Shaping the Progressive Movement

Roosevelt's presidency gave momentum to the Progressive movement, which sought to address the social and economic challenges of the industrial age through political reform. His advocacy for a more active federal government aligned with Progressive goals and helped bring these ideas into the mainstream of American politics.

Many of the reforms Roosevelt championed - such as the regulation of food and drugs, conservation of natural resources, and curbs on corporate power - became key planks in the Progressive platform. His success in implementing these policies demonstrated the potential for government action to address social and economic problems.

Roosevelt's influence extended beyond specific policies. His energetic style of leadership and his use of the presidency as a platform for advocating reform set a new standard for presidential activism. Future Progressive leaders, including his cousin Franklin D. Roosevelt, would draw inspiration from Theodore's example.

The New Nationalism

After leaving office, Roosevelt continued to shape progressive politics through his advocacy for what he called the "New Nationalism." This philosophy, which he outlined in a 1910 speech, called for an even more expansive role for the federal government in regulating the economy and promoting social welfare.

The New Nationalism proposed ideas that were radical for their time, such as a national health service, social insurance for the elderly, and more robust labor protections. While many of these proposals were not implemented during Roosevelt's lifetime, they foreshadowed later developments in American social policy.

Roosevelt's ideas about the concentration of wealth and the need for government to act as a counterweight to corporate power remain relevant in current debates about economic inequality and corporate influence in politics. His argument that the government should act to ensure a "square deal" for all citizens continues to resonate with many Americans.

Roosevelt's Enduring Influence

More than a century after his presidency, Roosevelt's ideas continue to influence American politics in numerous ways:

1. Environmental Policy: The modern environmental movement owes much to Roosevelt's conservation efforts. Debates about public land use, resource management, and the balance between conservation and development often reference Roosevelt's policies and philosophy.

2. Antitrust and Corporate Regulation: Roosevelt's approach to "trust-busting" and corporate regulation continues to inform discussions about market competition and corporate power. His nuanced view of regulating rather than simply breaking up large corporations remains relevant in an era of global conglomerates.

3. Consumer Protection: The principle that the government has a role in protecting consumers from unsafe products and fraudulent practices, established under Roosevelt, remains a key aspect of federal regulatory policy.

4. The Role of Government: Roosevelt's vision of an active federal government, willing to intervene in economic and social affairs to promote the public good, continues to be a touchstone in debates about the proper role of government in American society.

5. Presidential Leadership: Roosevelt's energetic use of presidential power and his concept of the presidency as a "bully pulpit" have influenced subsequent presidents and shaped public expectations of presidential leadership.

6. Progressive Taxation: Roosevelt's support for progressive taxation and his belief that great wealth carried social responsibilities continue to inform debates about tax policy and economic inequality.

7. Labor Relations: Roosevelt's efforts to balance the interests of workers and management set precedents for government involvement in labor disputes that continue to shape labor policy.

Lessons for Today's Leaders

Roosevelt's presidency offers valuable lessons for contemporary leaders:

1. The Power of Vision: Roosevelt had a clear vision for America and used his position to advocate for it tirelessly. His ability to articulate this vision and rally public support demonstrates the importance of clear, compelling leadership.

2. Balancing Interests: Roosevelt's "Square Deal" sought to balance the interests of various groups in society. This approach to governance, seeking fairness and compromise, remains relevant in our often polarized political climate.

3. Courage in Leadership: Roosevelt was willing to take on powerful interests when he believed it was in the public interest. His courage in facing down corporate monopolies and advocating for reforms offers an example of principled leadership.

4. The Importance of Communication: Roosevelt was a master communicator who used the presidency as a platform to speak directly to the American people. His skill in explaining complex issues and building public support for his policies highlights the importance of effective communication in leadership.

5. Adaptability: While Roosevelt had strong principles, he was also pragmatic and willing to adapt his approach as circumstances changed. This flexibility allowed him to achieve significant reforms in a changing political landscape.

As we face our own crossroads as a nation, struggling with issues of economic inequality, corporate power, environmental challenges, and the proper role of government, Roosevelt's legacy offers both inspiration and practical guidance. His vision of a government actively working to ensure a "square deal" for all citizens continues to shape our political discourse and challenge us to live up to our highest ideals as a nation.

Part III: Franklin D. Roosevelt - Steering Through Depression and War (1933 - 1945)

1. FDR's Privileged Upbringing

A Gilded Childhood at Hyde Park

On January 30, 1882, Franklin Delano Roosevelt entered the world at his family's estate in Hyde Park, New York. Born into one of America's most prominent families, young Franklin's early life was one of privilege and opportunity. The sprawling Springwood estate, with its grand mansion and expansive grounds, provided an idyllic setting for a childhood far removed from the hardships faced by many Americans of the era.

Franklin was the only child of James Roosevelt and Sara Delano Roosevelt. His father, a businessman and landowner, was 54 when Franklin was born, while his mother was 28. This age difference meant that Sara played a particularly dominant role in Franklin's upbringing, an influence that would continue well into his adult life.

The Roosevelt name carried significant weight in American society. Franklin's fifth cousin, Theodore Roosevelt, would become President of the United States when Franklin was just 19. This family connection to power and public service would shape Franklin's ambitions and outlook from an early age.

Life at Hyde Park was comfortable and structured. Young Franklin enjoyed the outdoors, developing a love for swimming, sailing, and bird watching that would stay with him throughout his life. He was also exposed to the world of politics and public affairs from an early age, as his father often discussed such matters at the dinner table.

Education of a Future President

Franklin's education began at home under the tutelage of private governesses and tutors. This early instruction instilled in him a love of learning and a broad curiosity about the world. It also allowed for a personalized education tailored to his interests and abilities. At the age of 14, Franklin was sent to Groton School, an elite preparatory school in Massachusetts. Groton, under the leadership of Reverend Endicott Peabody, emphasized not just academic excellence but also moral character and social responsibility. The school's motto, "Cui servire est regnare" (To serve is to rule), would have a lasting impact on Franklin's sense of duty and public service.

At Groton, Franklin was an average student academically but excelled in extracurricular activities. He edited the school magazine and was active in the debate club, honing skills that would serve him well in his future political career. The school also exposed him to ideas about social reform and the obligations of the privileged to help those less fortunate.

After Groton, Franklin attended Harvard College, following in the footsteps of many in his family. At Harvard, he continued to be more focused on social activities and networking than on academics. He joined the Alpha Delta Phi fraternity and was elected editor-in-chief of the Harvard Crimson newspaper.

Franklin's time at Harvard broadened his horizons and exposed him to a wider range of people and ideas. It was here that he began to develop his own political views, distinct from the conservative Republicanism of much of his family. He also honed his social skills and began to build the network of connections that would prove valuable in his later political career. After Harvard, Franklin attended Columbia Law School. Though he passed the bar exam in 1907, he never completed his law degree. His legal studies, however, provided him with a solid understanding of the law that would prove invaluable in his political career.

Influences on a Young Mind

Several key influences shaped Franklin's political philosophy during his formative years:

1. Family Legacy: The Roosevelt name and its association with public service had a significant impact on Franklin. The example of his cousin Theodore, in particular, inspired Franklin's interest in politics and progressive reform.

2. Sara Delano Roosevelt: Franklin's mother played a crucial role in shaping his character and ambitions. Her high expectations and support instilled in him a sense of confidence and duty.

3. Reverend Endicott Peabody: The headmaster of Groton School had a profound influence on Franklin's moral and ethical outlook. Peabody's emphasis on social responsibility and service to others resonated deeply with the young Roosevelt.

4. Progressive Era Ideas: Franklin came of age during the Progressive Era, a time of social activism and political reform. The ideas of progressive thinkers about using government to address social and economic issues would inform his later political philosophy.

5. Eleanor Roosevelt: Franklin's relationship with his fifth cousin once removed, whom he would later marry, exposed him to more progressive ideas about social reform and women's rights.

6. Travel: Franklin's family wealth allowed for extensive travel, including annual trips to Europe. These experiences broadened his worldview and gave him a more international perspective than many of his peers.

Shaping a Political Philosophy

As Franklin moved from childhood to young adulthood, his political philosophy began to take shape. While he came from a traditionally Republican family, he found himself increasingly drawn to the progressive wing of the Democratic Party.

Several factors contributed to this political evolution:

1. Social Conscience: His experiences at Groton and exposure to progressive ideas instilled in Franklin a strong sense of social responsibility. He began to see government as a potential force for positive change in society.

2. Admiration for Woodrow Wilson: As a young man, Franklin was impressed by Woodrow Wilson's scholarly approach to politics and his vision of an activist federal government. Wilson's New Freedom platform, with its emphasis on attacking concentrated economic power, resonated with Roosevelt.

3. Belief in Active Government: Unlike the laissez-faire approach favored by many of his class, Franklin came to believe that government should play an active role in addressing social and economic issues.

4. Internationalism: His travels and education gave Franklin a more global outlook. He saw America as having a role to play on the world stage, a view that would significantly influence his later foreign policy.

5. Pragmatism: Despite his idealistic streak, Franklin was also a pragmatist. He believed in working within the system to effect change, an approach that would characterize his later political career.

The Foundations of Leadership

Franklin's privileged upbringing provided him with many advantages, but it also instilled in him a sense of responsibility to use those advantages for the public good. His education, both formal and informal, equipped him with the skills and knowledge he would need to face the world of politics.

The confidence instilled in him by his mother, the moral grounding provided by his education at Groton, the social connections made at Harvard, and the legal knowledge gained at Columbia all contributed to the formation of the leader Franklin would become.

Yet, it would be a mistake to see Franklin's path to the presidency as predetermined by his privileged background. Many of his peers had similar advantages but did not achieve the same level of political success. What set Franklin apart was his ability to connect with people from all walks of life, his adaptability in the face of challenges, and his vision for what America could be.

As we follow Franklin's journey from the privileged child of Hyde Park to the President who would lead America through the Great Depression and World War II, we'll see how the influences of his youth shaped his approach to the monumental challenges he would face. We'll also see how he transcended his privileged background to become a champion for the common man, fundamentally reshaping the relationship between the American people and their government.

Franklin's story reminds us that leadership is not just about background or education, but about how one uses those advantages to serve others. It's a lesson in the power of empathy, vision, and adaptability - qualities that would serve Franklin well as he faced the greatest crisis of the 20th century.

2. Entry into Politics

The First Steps

Franklin D. Roosevelt's entry into politics was not a sudden leap but a gradual progression, fueled by ambition, family connections, and a genuine desire to serve. His political journey began in 1910 when he was elected to the New York State Senate, representing the 26th District.

At 28, FDR was a fresh face in Albany, but he quickly made his mark. He opposed the Tammany Hall political machine, a powerful Democratic organization known for its corrupt practices. This stance against entrenched political interests showcased Roosevelt's willingness to challenge the status quo, a trait that would define his later career.

During his time in the state senate, Roosevelt championed progressive causes. He advocated for conservation efforts, supported farmers' interests, and pushed for social welfare programs. These early political battles gave him valuable experience in coalition-building and legislative maneuvering.

Roosevelt's rising star caught the attention of national Democratic leaders. In 1912, he supported Woodrow Wilson's presidential campaign, a decision that would shape the next phase of his political career.

Assistant Secretary of the Navy

In 1913, newly elected President Wilson appointed Roosevelt as Assistant Secretary of the Navy. This position, which his cousin Theodore had once held, placed FDR at the heart of national politics and gave him his first taste of executive power.

As Assistant Secretary, Roosevelt threw himself into the job with characteristic energy. He oversaw the day-to-day operations of the Navy Department, gaining valuable administrative experience. He also became an advocate for a strong naval force, arguing that it was essential for America's security and global influence.

Roosevelt's time at the Navy Department coincided with World War I, providing him with firsthand experience in wartime administration. He played a key role in expanding the Navy, overseeing the quadrupling of Naval personnel and the significant increase in ship construction.

During this period, Roosevelt also honed his political skills. He learned to work within Washington's bureaucracy and built relationships with key political figures. His ability to work effectively with Congress and his skill in public relations served him well throughout his career.

In 1918, Roosevelt traveled to Europe to inspect naval installations. This trip gave him valuable insights into international affairs and the devastation caused by the war. It reinforced his belief in the need for American involvement in world affairs, a view that would shape his future foreign policy.

Roosevelt's tenure as Assistant Secretary ended in 1920, but the experience he gained would prove invaluable. He had learned the workings of the federal government, developed a network of political connections, and gained a national profile.

The 1920 Vice Presidential Campaign

In 1920, the Democratic Party chose Roosevelt as their vice-presidential nominee, running alongside presidential candidate James M. Cox. Although the ticket lost to Warren G. Harding in a landslide, the campaign gave Roosevelt national exposure and further political experience.

During the campaign, Roosevelt traveled extensively, making speeches across the country. This experience improved his public speaking skills and gave him a broader understanding of the nation's mood and concerns. Despite the loss, Roosevelt emerged from the campaign as a rising star in the Democratic Party.

The Setback and Comeback

Roosevelt's political career faced a significant challenge in 1921 when he contracted polio while vacationing in Canada. The disease left him paralyzed from the waist down, a condition that would have ended many political careers in that era.

However, Roosevelt refused to be defined by his disability. With the support of his wife Eleanor and his political advisor Louis Howe, he began the long process of rehabilitation while maintaining his political connections. This period of personal struggle strengthened Roosevelt's character and deepened his empathy for those facing hardship.

Return to Politics: The 1924 and 1928 Democratic Conventions

Roosevelt made his return to the national political stage at the 1924 Democratic National Convention. Despite still recovering from polio, he delivered a powerful speech nominating Al Smith for president. The speech, which Roosevelt delivered while supporting himself on crutches, demonstrated his resilience and reignited his political career.

In 1928, Roosevelt again nominated Smith at the Democratic Convention. This time, Smith won the nomination and asked Roosevelt to run for Governor of New York. Roosevelt initially hesitated, feeling he wasn't physically ready for the rigors of the campaign. However, with encouragement from Eleanor and Louis Howe, he accepted the challenge.

Governor of New York

Roosevelt's campaign for governor was a test of his political skills and physical endurance. He traveled extensively across the state, often appearing in public in a specially designed car that allowed him to speak from the backseat. His warm personality and optimistic message resonated with voters, and he won the election by a narrow margin.

As governor, Roosevelt faced significant challenges. The stock market crash of 1929 and the onset of the Great Depression hit New York hard. Roosevelt responded with a series of relief programs that foreshadowed his later New Deal policies. He expanded unemployment relief, initiated a public works program, and provided aid to farmers.

Roosevelt's governorship was marked by his willingness to experiment with new policies to address the economic crisis. He established the Temporary Emergency Relief Administration, the first state relief agency in the country. This program provided work for the unemployed and direct relief for those in need.

Another significant aspect of Roosevelt's governorship was his approach to power companies. He believed that electricity was a public necessity and should be affordable for all. He pushed for public development of hydroelectric power and stricter regulation of utility companies. This stance put him at odds with powerful business interests but gained him popular support. Roosevelt's time as governor also saw him develop his skills as a communicator. He began using radio addresses to speak directly to the people of New York, a technique he would later use to great effect as president.

Preparing for the Presidency

Roosevelt's governorship of New York was crucial in preparing him for the presidency. It gave him executive experience in managing a large, diverse state and dealing with the economic crisis. He learned to balance competing interests, work with the legislature, and implement innovative policies.

Moreover, his success in New York made him a leading contender for the Democratic presidential nomination in 1932. His record of progressive reforms and his ability to win in a large, diverse state made him an attractive candidate to many Democrats.

Roosevelt's experiences as governor also shaped his approach to the presidency. The relief programs he implemented in New York became models for his later New Deal policies. His battles with power companies informed his views on business regulation. His use of radio to communicate directly with voters foreshadowed his famous "fireside chats" as president.

Perhaps most importantly, Roosevelt's time as governor reinforced his belief in the power of government to improve people's lives. He saw firsthand the impact of the Depression on ordinary Americans and became convinced that bold action was needed to address the crisis.

As Roosevelt prepared to seek the presidency, he brought with him a wealth of experience from his early political career. From his time in the New York State Senate to his role as Assistant Secretary of the Navy to his governorship, he had gained a deep understanding of government at all levels. He had faced personal challenges that had strengthened his character and deepened his empathy.

Roosevelt's journey to this point had been marked by both privilege and adversity. He had used his advantages to serve others and had overcome significant obstacles. As he set his sights on the White House, he was ready to bring his experience, his optimism, and his vision for a better America to the national stage.

The lessons Roosevelt learned during his early political career would serve him well as he faced the enormous challenges of the presidency. His willingness to experiment with new policies, his skill in communicating with the public, and his belief in the power of government action would all play crucial roles in his response to the Great Depression and World War II.

3. The New Deal and Economic Recovery

A Nation in Crisis

When Franklin D. Roosevelt took office in March 1933, America was in the depths of the Great Depression. Banks were failing, unemployment had reached 25%, and hope was scarce. FDR's response to this crisis, the New Deal, would reshape the American government and society for generations to come.

Roosevelt's approach to the Great Depression was characterized by bold experimentation and a willingness to use federal power in unprecedented ways. His famous first inaugural address set the tone: "The only thing we have to fear is fear itself." With these words, FDR sought to restore confidence and hope to a demoralized nation.

The First Hundred Days

Roosevelt's first hundred days in office saw a flurry of activity as he and Congress worked to implement the first phase of the New

Deal. This period of intense legislative action set a standard against which future presidents would be measured.

Key initiatives of the First Hundred Days included:

1. The Emergency Banking Act: This law closed all banks for a "bank holiday," allowing only those deemed solvent to reopen. It helped restore confidence in the banking system.

2. The Federal Emergency Relief Administration (FERA): This program provided direct relief to the unemployed and their families.

3. The Civilian Conservation Corps (CCC): This program put young men to work on conservation projects, providing jobs and improving the nation's natural resources.

4. The Tennessee Valley Authority (TVA): This ambitious project aimed to provide electricity and promote economic development in the impoverished Tennessee Valley region.

5. The National Industrial Recovery Act (NIRA): This law established codes of fair competition for industries and guaranteed workers the right to unionize.

These and other measures demonstrated Roosevelt's commitment to using government power to address the economic crisis. They also showed his willingness to experiment with new approaches, even if it meant expanding federal authority in unprecedented ways.

The Second New Deal

As the Depression continued, Roosevelt launched a second wave of New Deal programs in 1935-1936. These initiatives focused more on long-term reform and social welfare.

Key components of the Second New Deal included:

1. The Social Security Act: This landmark legislation established a system of old-age pensions and unemployment insurance, creating a safety net for American workers.

2. The Wagner Act: Also known as the National Labor Relations Act, this law protected workers' rights to unionize and engage in collective bargaining.

3. The Works Progress Administration (WPA): This massive public works program employed millions of Americans in construction projects and cultural initiatives.

4. The Rural Electrification Administration (REA): This program brought electricity to rural areas, dramatically improving life for millions of farm families.

These programs further expanded the role of the federal government in American life and laid the groundwork for the modern welfare state.

Effectiveness of the New Deal

Assessing the effectiveness of the New Deal is a complex task. While it did not end the Great Depression – that would take the economic stimulus of World War II – it did bring significant relief to millions of Americans and implemented lasting reforms.

The New Deal's immediate impact was substantial:

1. It provided jobs for millions through programs like the CCC and WPA.

2. It stabilized the banking system and restored confidence in financial institutions.

3. It brought electricity and modern amenities to rural areas through the TVA and REA.

4. It established a social safety net through programs like Social Security.

Moreover, the New Deal had significant long-term effects:

1. It reshaped the relationship between the federal government and citizens, establishing an expectation that the government would play an active role in ensuring economic security.

2. It strengthened the labor movement, leading to improved working conditions and wages for many Americans.

3. It implemented regulations on the financial industry that helped prevent another depression for decades.

4. It left a lasting physical legacy through public works projects, many of which are still in use today.

However, the New Deal also faced criticism. Some argued that it didn't go far enough in addressing economic inequality, while others felt it gave too much power to the federal government. The Supreme Court struck down some New Deal programs as unconstitutional, leading to FDR's controversial (and ultimately unsuccessful) attempt to "pack" the court.

FDR's Approach to the Great Depression

Roosevelt's approach to the Great Depression was characterized by several key elements:

1. Experimentation: FDR was willing to try new ideas and abandon those that didn't work. He famously said, "It is common sense to take a method and try it. If it fails, admit it frankly and try another. But above all, try something."

2. Direct government intervention: Unlike his predecessor, Herbert Hoover, who believed in limited government action, FDR saw an active role for the government in addressing economic crises.

3. Focus on relief, recovery, and reform: The New Deal aimed not just to provide immediate relief, but also to implement long-term reforms to prevent future crises.

4. Communication: FDR used his "fireside chats" to explain his policies directly to the American people, building public support for his programs.

5. Pragmatism: While guided by progressive ideals, Roosevelt was also pragmatic, willing to work with business leaders and conservatives when necessary to achieve his goals.

This approach represented a significant shift in American governance. It expanded the power and scope of the federal government, established new expectations for presidential leadership, and created a new relationship between citizens and their government.

Long-Term Impact of the New Deal

The impact of the New Deal extended far beyond the 1930s. It fundamentally altered American politics and society in ways that continue to shape our nation today:

1. The role of government: The New Deal established the idea that the federal government has a responsibility to ensure the economic well-being of its citizens. This principle has informed debates about the government's role ever since.

2. The Democratic coalition: The New Deal helped create a coalition of urban workers, farmers, intellectuals, and later, civil rights activists, that formed the base of the Democratic Party for decades.

3. The regulatory state: Many New Deal agencies and regulations, such as the Securities and Exchange Commission (SEC), continue to play important roles in regulating the economy.

4. Social welfare: Programs like Social Security laid the foundation for later expansions of the social safety net, including Medicare and Medicaid.

5. Labor rights: The Wagner Act and other New Deal labor laws strengthened the union movement, leading to improved conditions for workers in the post-war era.

6. Environmental conservation: The CCC and other New Deal conservation efforts set precedents for later environmental protection measures.

7. Infrastructure: New Deal public works projects built roads, bridges, schools, and other infrastructure that supported economic growth for generations.

The New Deal also had a lasting impact on American political culture. It popularized the idea that the government could and should play an active role in managing the economy and providing for citizens' welfare. This idea, while still debated, has remained a central part of American political discourse.

Lessons for Today

As we face our own economic challenges in the 21st century, the New Deal offers valuable lessons:

1. The importance of bold action in times of crisis: FDR's willingness to experiment and take decisive action helped restore confidence and hope.

2. The power of effective communication: Roosevelt's ability to explain complex policies in simple terms helped build public support for his programs.

3. The value of a comprehensive approach: The New Deal addressed not just immediate economic needs but also long-term structural issues.

4. The need for flexibility: FDR's willingness to adapt and try new approaches when initial efforts failed is a model for effective crisis management.

5. The potential for government to drive positive change: While the proper role of government remains debated, the New Deal demonstrated the government's capacity to address large-scale societal challenges.

As we continue to battle with issues of economic inequality, financial regulation, and the proper role of government, the New Deal remains a touchstone. Its successes and shortcomings continue to inform our debates about how best to ensure prosperity and security for all Americans.

The story of the New Deal reminds us that in times of crisis, bold leadership and a willingness to innovate can make a real difference in people's lives. It challenges us to think creatively about how to address our own economic and social challenges, always keeping in mind FDR's commitment to the "forgotten man at the bottom of the economic pyramid."

4. World War II Leadership

The Road to War

As the 1930s progressed, Franklin D. Roosevelt found himself increasingly focused on events abroad. The rise of fascism in Europe and Japanese aggression in Asia posed growing threats to world peace. FDR, with his internationalist outlook, recognized the danger these developments posed to American security and interests.

Initially, Roosevelt had to balance his concern about foreign threats with the strong isolationist sentiment in the United States. Many Americans, remembering the costs of World War I, were determined to avoid entanglement in another European conflict. This sentiment was reflected in neutrality laws passed by Congress in the 1930s.

Roosevelt skillfully navigated these constraints, gradually preparing the nation for the possibility of war while respecting the public's desire for peace. He used his fireside chats to educate Americans about international events and the potential consequences of isolationism.

Key decisions in the lead-up to war included:

1. The "Quarantine Speech" (1937): Roosevelt called for economic pressure on aggressive nations, likening the spread of war to a contagious disease that needed to be contained.

2. "Cash and Carry" (1939): This policy allowed the sale of military supplies to nations at war, as long as they paid cash and transported the goods themselves. It primarily benefited Britain and France.

3. Destroyer-for-Bases Deal (1940): Roosevelt traded 50 outdated destroyers to Britain in exchange for leases on British bases in the Western Hemisphere.

4. Lend-Lease Act (1941): This program allowed the U.S. to supply Allied nations with war materials without technically entering the conflict.

These measures demonstrated Roosevelt's ability to find creative solutions to complex problems, gradually moving the nation toward greater involvement in world affairs while respecting legal and political constraints.

Pearl Harbor and America's Entry into War

The Japanese attack on Pearl Harbor on December 7, 1941, dramatically altered the situation. Roosevelt's response to this crisis showcased his leadership skills. His address to Congress the next day, asking for a declaration of war against Japan, is a masterpiece of political rhetoric. The famous opening line, "Yesterday, December 7, 1941 - a date which will live in infamy," set the tone for America's entry into World War II.

Roosevelt's decision to focus first on defeating Germany, despite the attack coming from Japan, was a key strategic choice. This "Germany First" policy, agreed upon with British Prime Minister Winston Churchill, recognized that Nazi Germany posed the greater threat to global security.

Wartime Leadership

As Commander-in-Chief, Roosevelt displayed remarkable leadership qualities:

1. Strategic Vision: Roosevelt understood the global nature of the conflict and the need for a comprehensive Allied strategy. He worked closely with Churchill and later Soviet leader Joseph Stalin to coordinate war efforts.

2. Delegation: FDR appointed capable individuals to key positions and gave them the authority to act. His selection of General George Marshall as Army Chief of Staff and his trust in General Dwight D. Eisenhower as Supreme Allied Commander in Europe were particularly significant.

3. Communication: Roosevelt continued to use his fireside chats to inform and rally the American people. His ability to explain complex situations in simple terms helped maintain public support for the war effort.

4. Decision-making: FDR showed a willingness to make tough decisions. The internment of Japanese Americans, while now recognized as a grave injustice, demonstrated his readiness to take controversial actions he believed necessary for national security.

5. Innovation: Roosevelt supported the development of new technologies, including the atomic bomb. The Manhattan Project, conducted in strict secrecy, showcased his ability to manage large-scale, cutting-edge scientific endeavors.

Home Front Leadership

Roosevelt's leadership extended beyond military strategy to managing the home front. Key initiatives included:

1. War Production Board: This agency oversaw the conversion of American industry to war production, resulting in a staggering output of military equipment.

2. Office of Price Administration: This body regulated prices and rationing to prevent inflation and ensure fair distribution of scarce resources.

3. War Labor Board: This agency mediated labor disputes to maintain industrial productivity.

4. Office of War Information: This organization managed propaganda and public information about the war effort.

These measures demonstrated Roosevelt's understanding that total war required mobilization of the entire society. His leadership helped transform America into what he called the "Arsenal of Democracy," producing the material needed for Allied victory.

Diplomacy and Alliance Management

Roosevelt's wartime diplomacy was crucial to Allied success. He forged and maintained the Grand Alliance with Britain and the Soviet Union, despite the significant ideological differences between these nations.

Key diplomatic achievements included:

1. Atlantic Charter (1941): This joint declaration with Churchill outlined Allied goals for the post-war world, including self-determination for all peoples and freer trade.

2. Tehran Conference (1943): This first meeting of Roosevelt, Churchill, and Stalin coordinated military strategy and began discussions on the post-war order.

3. Bretton Woods Conference (1944): This meeting established the framework for the post-war international monetary system, including the creation of the International Monetary Fund and the World Bank.

4. Yalta Conference (1945): This final meeting of the Big Three leaders made crucial decisions about the post-war division of Europe and the establishment of the United Nations.

Roosevelt's diplomatic skills were evident in his ability to maintain unity among the Allies while also advancing American interests. He balanced the need to work with Stalin against his concerns about Soviet expansionism, laying the groundwork for the post-war containment policy.

Vision for the Post-War World

Roosevelt's vision for the post-war world was shaped by his internationalist outlook and his belief in American leadership. Key elements of this vision included:

1. United Nations: FDR was a driving force behind the creation of this international organization, seeing it as essential for maintaining world peace.

2. Decolonization: Roosevelt supported the principle of self-determination for colonized peoples, often to the chagrin of America's European allies.

3. International Economic Cooperation: The Bretton Woods system reflected Roosevelt's belief in the need for stable international economic relations to prevent future conflicts.

4. Four Freedoms: In his 1941 State of the Union address, Roosevelt articulated four fundamental freedoms - freedom of speech, freedom of worship, freedom from want, and freedom from fear - that he believed should be universal human rights.

This vision represented a dramatic shift in America's role in the world. Roosevelt saw the United States not just as a military superpower, but as a leader in shaping a new international order based on cooperation and shared prosperity.

Legacy in International Relations

Roosevelt's wartime leadership and his vision for the post-war world had a lasting impact on international relations:

1. American Global Leadership: FDR's policies established the United States as the leader of the free world, a position it would maintain throughout the Cold War and beyond.

2. International Institutions: The United Nations, the International Monetary Fund, and the World Bank continue to play significant roles in global governance.

3. Collective Security: The principle of collective security, embodied in the UN Charter, remains a cornerstone of international relations.

4. Human Rights: The Four Freedoms and the Atlantic Charter influenced the development of international human rights law, including the Universal Declaration of Human Rights.

5. Containment Policy: While Roosevelt sought cooperation with the Soviet Union, his wariness of Stalin's intentions laid the groundwork for the containment policy that would define the Cold War era.

Roosevelt's approach to international relations - combining idealism with pragmatism, and assertive leadership with coalition-building - set a standard for American foreign policy that would influence his successors for decades to come.

Lessons for Today

Roosevelt's wartime leadership offers valuable lessons for modern leaders:

1. The importance of clear communication in times of crisis.

2. The need for flexibility and innovation in the face of unprecedented challenges.

3. The value of building and maintaining strong alliances.

4. The power of articulating a compelling vision for the future.

5. The necessity of balancing short-term needs with long-term goals.

As we face our own global challenges - from climate change to international terrorism - Roosevelt's example reminds us of the difference strong, principled leadership can make. His ability to guide the nation through the dual crises of the Great Depression and World War II, while also planning for a better post-war world, stands as powerful evidence of the potential of visionary leadership.

Roosevelt's presidency expanded the boundaries of what Americans believed their government could achieve, both at home and abroad. His leadership during World War II not only secured Allied victory but also positioned the United States as a global superpower with a responsibility to shape world affairs.

Reflecting on Roosevelt's wartime leadership, we're reminded of the enormous challenges he faced and the courage and vision he displayed in meeting them. His story is a powerful example of how leaders can rise to meet the greatest tests of their time, leaving a lasting impact on their nation and the world.

Part IV: Lyndon B. Johnson - The Path from Texas to Washington

1. Johnson's Roots and Education

The Hill Country's Son

On August 27, 1908, in a small farmhouse near Stonewall, Texas, Lyndon Baines Johnson entered the world. The Texas Hill Country, with its rugged terrain and hardscrabble farms, would shape the future president in ways that echoed throughout his life and political career.

LBJ, as he would come to be known, was born into a family with deep Texas roots and a tradition of public service. His father, Sam Ealy Johnson Jr., was a farmer and five-term member of the Texas legislature. His mother, Rebekah Baines Johnson, was a college graduate - unusual for women of her time - who instilled in her children a love of learning and high ambitions.

The Johnson family's circumstances were modest, but not impoverished. They lived in a small farmhouse without electricity or indoor plumbing - conveniences that wouldn't reach much of rural Texas until years later. Young Lyndon's childhood was marked by the rhythms of farm life: helping with chores, tending to livestock, and experiencing firsthand the unpredictability of agricultural fortunes.

These early years in the Hill Country left an indelible mark on Johnson. The stark beauty of the landscape, the tight-knit community spirit, and the ever-present challenges of rural life all contributed to shaping his worldview. Johnson would later recall these years with a mixture of nostalgia and determination, often referring to his humble origins as he advocated for policies to help the rural poor.

Education: A Ticket to a Broader World

From an early age, Lyndon showed signs of the ambition and drive that would characterize his later political career. His mother, recognizing her son's potential, pushed him to excel in his studies. Despite the limitations of rural schools, Johnson was an eager learner, often reading by kerosene lamp late into the night.

Johnson's formal education began in a one-room schoolhouse near the family farm. Here, he got his first taste of public speaking and leadership, often organizing games and activities for his fellow students. Even at this young age, Johnson displayed a knack for persuasion and an ability to rally others around him - skills that would serve him well in his future political career.

As he grew older, Johnson's educational journey took him further from home. He attended Johnson City High School, where he continued to excel academically and in extracurricular activities. It was here that Johnson began to dream of a life beyond the Hill Country, seeing education as his ticket to a broader world.

After graduating from high school in 1924, Johnson took a year off to work odd jobs and save money for college. This experience, working alongside people struggling to make ends meet, deepened his understanding of economic hardship and reinforced his determination to seek a better life through education.

In 1927, Johnson enrolled at Southwest Texas State Teachers College (now Texas State University) in San Marcos. This move marked a significant step in Johnson's life, exposing him to a wider range of ideas and experiences. At college, Johnson threw himself into campus life, joining debate teams, working on the college newspaper, and involving himself in student politics.

It was during his college years that Johnson got his first taste of teaching, working with Mexican-American children at the Welhausen School in Cotulla, Texas. This experience had a profound impact on Johnson, opening his eyes to the realities of poverty and discrimination faced by many Americans. Years later, as President, he would recall this time when signing major education and civil rights legislation.

The Impact of Poverty

While Johnson's family was not among the poorest in their community, they experienced periods of financial hardship that left a lasting impression on the young Lyndon. The boom-and-bust cycle of farming, coupled with his father's occasional business failures, meant that the Johnson family sometimes struggled to make ends meet.

One particularly difficult period came when Johnson was in his teens. His father made a series of poor investments that left the family deep in debt. Young Lyndon watched as his parents struggled to keep the farm, an experience that instilled in him a lifelong fear of poverty and a determination to achieve financial security.

These early brushes with economic insecurity had a huge impact on Johnson's political philosophy. They fostered in him a deep empathy for those struggling to get by and a belief in the power of government to improve people's lives. This perspective would later manifest in Johnson's ambitious "War on Poverty" and his vision of a "Great Society."

Johnson's experiences also gave him a firsthand understanding of the transformative power of federal initiatives. He saw how New Deal programs, particularly rural electrification, dramatically improved life in the Hill Country. This observation reinforced his belief in the positive role government could play in people's lives - a belief that would become a cornerstone of his political career.

The Making of a Politician

Even as a young man, Lyndon Johnson displayed many of the traits that would define his political career. He was ambitious, hardworking, and possessed an almost supernatural ability to read people and situations. These skills, honed in the close-knit communities of the Hill Country, would serve him well as he climbed the political ladder.

Johnson's upbringing also instilled in him a certain toughness and resilience. Life in the Hill Country was not easy, and Johnson learned early on the value of persistence in hard times. This quality would become evident in his political career, particularly in his dogged pursuit of legislative goals.

At the same time, Johnson's background gave him a genuine connection to the struggles of ordinary Americans. Unlike some politicians who came from privileged backgrounds, Johnson could speak authentically about poverty and hardship because he had experienced them firsthand. This authenticity would become a powerful tool in his political arsenal, allowing him to connect with voters and fellow politicians alike.

The Texas Imprint

Johnson's Texas roots influenced not just his political views, but his entire approach to politics. The rough-and-tumble nature of Texas politics, with its emphasis on personal relationships and deal-making, shaped Johnson's political style. He became known for his "Johnson Treatment" - a blend of persuasion, intimidation, and charm that he used to bend others to his will.

Moreover, Johnson's Texas background gave him a unique perspective on national issues. He often saw himself as a bridge between the South and the rest of the country, understanding both the conservative traditions of his home state and the need for progress on issues like civil rights and poverty alleviation.

Johnson's upbringing in the Hill Country also influenced his communication style. He had a gift for speaking in a direct, folksy manner that resonated with many Americans. His ability to simplify complex issues and relate them to everyday experiences was a skill honed in the small towns and farms of his youth.

2. Ascent in Congress

First Steps on Capitol Hill

Lyndon B. Johnson's journey to the halls of Congress began in 1937 when he won a special election to represent Texas's 10th congressional district. At just 28 years old, Johnson was one of the youngest members of the House of Representatives. His victory showcased his political acumen and his ability to connect with voters, traits that would serve him well throughout his career.

From the moment he arrived in Washington, Johnson displayed an uncommon drive and ambition. He worked tirelessly, often putting in 18-hour days, and quickly gained a reputation as a rising star in the Democratic Party. Johnson's work ethic was legendary; he often told his staff, "There are 24 hours in a day, and you can use all of them."

Johnson's early years in the House were marked by his close relationship with President Franklin D. Roosevelt. The young congressman saw in FDR a model of activist government that aligned with his own views. Johnson worked hard to bring New Deal programs to his district, understanding firsthand how federal initiatives could improve the lives of rural Americans.

Building a Power Base

In the House, Johnson quickly learned the importance of building alliances and accumulating power. He cultivated relationships with influential members of Congress, particularly House Speaker Sam Rayburn, another Texan who became Johnson's mentor and patron.

Johnson's political skills were on full display during his time in the House. He had an uncanny ability to read people, to understand their motivations and desires. This skill, combined with his relentless energy and ambition, allowed him to quickly climb the ranks of the Democratic Party.

One of Johnson's key strengths was his ability to build coalitions. He could bring together diverse groups, finding common ground and brokering compromises. This skill would prove invaluable as he rose to positions of greater power and responsibility.

The Senate Years Begin

In 1948, Johnson made the leap to the Senate in a hotly contested and controversial election. The race was so close that it earned Johnson the nickname "Landslide Lyndon" - he won by just 87 votes out of nearly a million cast. The election was marred by accusations of fraud, a cloud that would hang over Johnson for years to come.

Despite the controversy, Johnson arrived in the Senate ready to make his mark. He quickly set about building relationships and accumulating power, much as he had done in the House. Johnson's work ethic, his political savvy, and his ability to maneuver behind the scenes soon made him a force to be reckoned with in the Senate.

The Making of a Master Legislator

Johnson's rise in the Senate was meteoric. By 1951, just three years after joining the body, he had become the Democratic whip. Two years later, at the age of 44, he became the youngest Minority Leader in Senate history. When the Democrats regained control of the Senate in 1955, Johnson ascended to the position of Majority Leader.

As Majority Leader, Johnson truly came into his own as a political operator. He transformed the role, turning what had been a largely ceremonial position into one of real power and influence. Johnson used his position to control the flow of legislation, deciding which bills would come to the floor and when.

Johnson's leadership style was characterized by what became known as the "Johnson Treatment." This was his unique blend of persuasion, intimidation, and charm that he used to bend others to his will. Johnson would tower over other senators, invading their personal space, alternately cajoling and threatening until he got what he wanted.

One senator described the Johnson Treatment this way: "It was an incredible, potent mixture of persuasion, badgering, flattery, threats, reminders of past favors and future advantages." Johnson's physical presence - he stood 6'4" and wasn't afraid to use his size to intimidate - was a key part of his political arsenal.

Master of the Senate

Johnson's tenure as Senate Majority Leader was marked by significant legislative achievements. He played a key role in passing the Civil Rights Act of 1957, the first civil rights legislation since Reconstruction. While the bill was watered down to secure passage, it represented a crucial first step in the long struggle for civil rights.

Johnson's skill as a legislator was perhaps best exemplified by his handling of the 1958 National Aeronautics and Space Act, which created NASA. Johnson managed to bridge the divide between those who wanted a civilian agency and those who preferred military control, crafting a compromise that allowed the bill to pass.

Johnson's ability to get things done in the Senate was rooted in his deep understanding of the institution and its members. He kept a detailed ledger of favors owed and given, and he wasn't afraid to call in those favors when he needed votes. Johnson once said, "I do understand power, whatever else may be said about me. I know where to look for it, and how to use it."

The Significance of Johnson's Senate Leadership

Johnson's time as Senate Majority Leader was significant for several reasons. First, it demonstrated his exceptional political skills. Johnson's ability to count votes, to know exactly where each senator stood on an issue and what it would take to change their mind, was unparalleled.

Second, Johnson's leadership style transformed the role of Majority Leader. He centralized power in the position, making it second only to the presidency in terms of influence over domestic policy. This change would have lasting effects on how the Senate operated.

Third, Johnson's tenure saw the passage of significant legislation, from civil rights to space exploration. These achievements set the stage for the more ambitious legislative agenda he would pursue as president.

Finally, Johnson's time as Majority Leader burnished his reputation as a master politician. His ability to get things done, to forge compromises and build coalitions, made him a formidable figure in Washington. This reputation would serve him well when he became vice president and later president.

Lessons in Leadership

Johnson's rise in Congress offers several valuable lessons in leadership:

1. The Power of Relationships: Johnson understood that personal relationships were the currency of politics. He invested time and energy in building and maintaining these relationships, knowing they would pay dividends in the future.

2. Know Your Institution: Johnson's success was rooted in his deep understanding of how Congress worked. He knew the rules, both written and unwritten, and used this knowledge to his advantage.

3. Work Ethic Matters: Johnson's legendary work ethic set him apart from his peers. He outworked everyone around him, often putting in 18-hour days.

4. Adaptability is Key: Johnson was able to adapt his approach based on the situation and the people he was dealing with. He could be charming or intimidating, whatever the situation called for.

5. Vision and Detail: Johnson combined big-picture thinking with attention to detail. He had a vision for what he wanted to accomplish, but he also understood the nitty-gritty details needed to make it happen.

Johnson's rise to power came at a cost. His relentless ambition and his willingness to use any means necessary to achieve his goals earned him many enemies. Some saw him as ruthless and unprincipled, willing to do anything to accumulate and maintain power.

Moreover, the stress of his position took a toll on Johnson's health. He smoked heavily, drank too much, and suffered a severe heart attack in 1955. The experience shook Johnson and led him to briefly consider leaving politics.

But Johnson's ambition would not let him quit. He returned to the Senate with renewed vigor, setting his sights on an even bigger prize: the presidency. Johnson's time in the Senate had prepared him well for this next challenge. He had honed his political skills, built a national reputation, and demonstrated his ability to get things done in Washington.

3. The Great Society and Vietnam

A Vision for America

When Lyndon B. Johnson ascended to the presidency following the tragic assassination of John F. Kennedy in November 1963, he brought with him a bold vision for America. This vision, which he called the "Great Society," was rooted in Johnson's experiences growing up in the Texas Hill Country and his years observing poverty and inequality as a politician.

In a speech at the University of Michigan in May 1964, Johnson outlined his vision: "The Great Society rests on abundance and liberty for all. It demands an end to poverty and racial injustice." With these words, Johnson set in motion one of the most ambitious domestic agendas in American history.

The Great Society: Goals and Programs

Johnson's Great Society aimed to eliminate poverty, reduce inequality, improve education, rejuvenate cities, and protect the environment. It was, in many ways, an extension and expansion of Franklin D. Roosevelt's New Deal, adapted for the challenges of the 1960s.

Some of the key programs and initiatives of the Great Society included:

1. The War on Poverty: This umbrella term encompassed various programs aimed at reducing poverty in America. It included the creation of Medicare and Medicaid, which provided health coverage for the elderly and the poor, respectively. The Food Stamp program was expanded, and new initiatives like Head Start, which provided early education for disadvantaged children, were launched.

2. Education Reform: Johnson, a former teacher, placed a high priority on education. The Elementary and Secondary Education Act of 1965 provided federal funding to K-12 schools, particularly those serving low-income students. The Higher Education Act of the same year increased federal money given to universities and created scholarships and low-interest loans for students.

3. Civil Rights: Building on the momentum of the Civil Rights Movement, Johnson pushed through landmark legislation including the Civil Rights Act of 1964 and the Voting Rights Act of 1965. These laws outlawed discrimination based on race, color, religion, sex, or national origin and ensured voting rights for African Americans.

4. Urban Development: Programs like Model Cities aimed to rejuvenate urban areas through coordinated federal, state, and local efforts. The Department of Housing and Urban Development was created to oversee these initiatives.

5. Environmental Protection: Johnson signed multiple environmental protection acts, including the Wilderness Act, the Land and Water Conservation Fund Act, and the Clean Air Act.

Outcomes of the Great Society

The impact of the Great Society programs was significant and far-reaching. The poverty rate, which stood at around 19% when Johnson took office, fell to 12.8% by 1968. Millions of elderly Americans received health coverage through Medicare, while Medicaid provided healthcare to low-income individuals. The Food Stamp program dramatically reduced hunger in America.

In education, federal funding for public schools more than doubled between 1965 and 1966. By the end of the decade, nearly half of all African American children were enrolled in Head Start programs. The Higher Education Act opened college doors to millions of Americans who might otherwise have been unable to afford it.

The civil rights legislation of this period transformed American society, outlawing segregation and discrimination in public accommodations, employment, and voting. While these laws didn't immediately end racism or inequality, they provided crucial legal tools for fighting discrimination.

Environmental initiatives protected millions of acres of wilderness and set the stage for future environmental regulations. The creation of the National Endowment for the Arts and the National Endowment for the Humanities supported American culture and scholarship in unprecedented ways.

However, the Great Society also faced criticism. Some argued that it expanded the federal government too much, while others felt it didn't go far enough in addressing systemic inequalities. The programs were expensive, contributing to inflation and budget deficits. Some initiatives, particularly in urban development, had unintended consequences and were less successful than hoped.

Despite these criticisms, the Great Society represented a high-water mark of liberal governance in post-war America. Many of its programs, like Medicare and Head Start, remain popular and important parts of the American social safety net today.

The Shadow of Vietnam

While Johnson was launching his ambitious domestic agenda, storm clouds were gathering over Southeast Asia. The Vietnam War, which had begun as a limited engagement under Eisenhower and Kennedy, would come to dominate Johnson's presidency and ultimately derail his Great Society.

Johnson inherited a deteriorating situation in Vietnam. The South Vietnamese government, which the U.S. supported, was losing ground to communist forces from North Vietnam and their allies in the South, known as the Viet Cong. Johnson faced a difficult choice: escalate American involvement or risk a communist takeover of South Vietnam.

Escalation and the Gulf of Tonkin

In August 1964, Johnson seized on reports of North Vietnamese attacks on American ships in the Gulf of Tonkin to secure congressional authorization for military action. The Gulf of Tonkin Resolution gave Johnson broad powers to conduct military operations in Southeast Asia without a formal declaration of war.

Johnson used this authority to gradually escalate American involvement in Vietnam. In 1965, he initiated a bombing campaign against North Vietnam and began deploying large numbers of U.S. ground troops to South Vietnam. By the end of the year, there were 184,000 American troops in Vietnam; by 1968, that number would reach over 500,000.

Johnson's handling of the war was characterized by a belief that gradual escalation could force North Vietnam to the negotiating table. He was determined to find a middle ground between withdrawal and all-out war. This strategy of "graduated pressure" satisfied neither hawks nor doves and ultimately proved ineffective against a determined enemy willing to absorb enormous losses.

The Costs of War

As the war dragged on, its costs - both human and financial - mounted. American casualties increased, with 1968 becoming the deadliest year of the war for U.S. forces. The financial burden of the war made it increasingly difficult for Johnson to fund his Great

Society programs. Moreover, the war began to tear at the fabric of American society. Anti-war protests grew in size and intensity, particularly on college campuses. The draft, which disproportionately affected lower-income and minority communities, became a focal point of discontent.

Television brought the brutal reality of the war into American living rooms in unprecedented ways. Images of combat and casualties eroded public support for the war and raised questions about its morality and purpose.

Johnson's Dilemma

As the war escalated, Johnson found himself in an increasingly untenable position. He was committed to preventing a communist takeover of South Vietnam, believing in the "domino theory" that if Vietnam fell, other countries in Southeast Asia would follow. At the same time, he was deeply invested in his domestic agenda and worried about the war's impact on the Great Society.

Johnson's public statements about the war often contrasted sharply with the reality on the ground, leading to what became known as the "credibility gap." His administration's optimistic pronouncements about the progress of the war were undermined by events like the Tet Offensive in early 1968, when North Vietnamese and Viet Cong forces launched a massive, coordinated attack across South Vietnam. While the Tet Offensive was ultimately a military failure for the communist forces, it was a psychological victory. It shattered the illusion that the U.S. was close to winning the war and further eroded public support for the conflict.

The Decision Not to Run

By early 1968, Johnson was a beleaguered president. The war had become a quagmire, with no clear path to victory. His Great Society programs, while achieving significant successes, were being undermined by the financial and political costs of the war. Johnson's approval ratings had plummeted, and he faced challenges from within his own party for the Democratic nomination.

On March 31, 1968, Johnson shocked the nation by announcing that he would not seek re-election. In a televised address, he stated: "I shall not seek, and I will not accept, the nomination of my party for another term as your President." With these words, Johnson effectively ended his political career.

Legacy of War and Peace

Johnson's presidency presents a study in contrasts. On the domestic front, his Great Society programs represented one of the most ambitious and far-reaching attempts to use federal power to address social issues in American history. Many of these programs continue to shape American society today.

On foreign policy, however, Johnson's legacy is dominated by the tragedy of Vietnam. His escalation of the war led to tens of thousands of American deaths and hundreds of thousands of Vietnamese casualties. The war's financial costs undermined the Great Society and contributed to economic challenges in the 1970s.

The Vietnam War also had profound effects on American politics and society. It fueled distrust in government, contributed to social unrest, and shaped a generation's worldview. The war's aftermath influenced American foreign policy for decades, creating a reluctance to engage in prolonged overseas military interventions that became known as the "Vietnam Syndrome."

Johnson's handling of Vietnam raises important questions about the limits of American power, the challenges of fighting a limited war against a determined adversary, and the difficulties of balancing domestic and foreign policy priorities.

4. Johnson's Impact on American Politics

A Legacy Written in Law

Lyndon B. Johnson's presidency left an indelible mark on American politics and society. His legislative achievements, particularly in civil rights, reshaped the nation's social landscape. The long-term effects of his domestic and foreign policies continue to reverberate through American life today.

The Civil Rights Triumph

Johnson's most enduring legacy may be his role in advancing civil rights. As Senate Majority Leader, he had helped pass the Civil Rights Act of 1957, the first such legislation since Reconstruction. But it was as president that Johnson truly made his mark on civil rights.

The Civil Rights Act of 1964 stands as one of the most significant pieces of legislation in American history. This sweeping law prohibited discrimination based on race, color, religion, sex, or national origin. It outlawed segregation in public places, banned employment discrimination, and paved the way for integration of schools and other public facilities.

Johnson's skill as a legislator was on full display as he maneuvered the Civil Rights Act through Congress. He used every tool at his disposal - persuasion, arm-twisting, appeals to conscience, and raw political power. His famous "Johnson Treatment" was applied liberally as he cajoled, threatened, and bargained with lawmakers to secure the votes needed for passage.

The Voting Rights Act of 1965 followed, addressing the barriers that had long prevented African Americans from exercising their right to vote. This law banned discriminatory voting practices such as literacy tests and provided for federal oversight of voter registration in areas with a history of discrimination.

These laws fundamentally altered the American political landscape. They empowered millions of African Americans to participate fully in the democratic process, reshaping electoral politics and paving the way for increased representation at all levels of government. Johnson's commitment to civil rights came at a political cost. As he signed the Civil Rights Act, he reportedly told an aide, "We have lost the South for a generation." This prediction proved accurate, as the Democratic Party's stronghold on the South began to crumble, reshaping the electoral map in ways that continue to influence American politics today.

Beyond Civil Rights: A Domestic Revolution

While civil rights legislation stands as Johnson's most celebrated achievement, his impact on domestic policy extended far beyond this realm. The sheer breadth and depth of Johnson's domestic agenda is staggering.

Medicare and Medicaid, cornerstones of Johnson's Great Society, fundamentally altered the American healthcare system. These programs provided health coverage for the elderly and the poor, respectively, marking the largest expansion of government-funded healthcare in U.S. history. Today, these programs serve millions of Americans and have become deeply embedded in the nation's social fabric.

Education was another area where Johnson left a lasting imprint. The Elementary and Secondary Education Act of 1965 dramatically increased federal funding for education, particularly for schools serving low-income students. This law established the federal government's role in K-12 education, a role that continues to evolve and spark debate today. The Higher Education Act of 1965 expanded federal aid to colleges and universities and created federal scholarships and low-interest loan programs for students. This legislation opened the doors of higher education to millions of Americans who might otherwise have been unable to afford college.

Johnson's War on Poverty, while not achieving its lofty goal of eliminating poverty, did make significant strides. Programs like Head Start, which provides early education for disadvantaged children, and the expansion of the Food Stamp program (now known as SNAP) helped reduce poverty rates and continue to provide crucial support for low-income Americans.

Environmental protection was another area where Johnson left a lasting legacy. Laws like the Wilderness Act, the Land and Water Conservation Fund Act, and the Clean Air Act laid the groundwork for modern environmental regulation and conservation efforts.

Long-Term Effects: Reshaping Government's Role

Johnson's domestic policies fundamentally altered the relationship between the federal government and the American people. The Great Society programs expanded the government's role in areas like healthcare, education, and poverty alleviation. This expansion of federal power has been a source of ongoing political debate, with supporters arguing for the necessity of these programs and critics warning of government overreach.

The financial impact of these programs has also been significant. While they have provided crucial support for millions of Americans, they have also contributed to increased government spending and debates over fiscal policy that continue to this day.

Johnson's domestic agenda also set the stage for future policy debates. Issues like healthcare reform, education policy, and the proper role of government in addressing social issues continue to dominate political discourse, with the programs and principles established during Johnson's presidency often serving as key reference points.

Foreign Policy: The Shadow of Vietnam

While Johnson's domestic achievements were numerous and far-reaching, his foreign policy legacy is dominated by the Vietnam War. The war's impact on American politics and society was profound and long-lasting. The escalation of the war under Johnson led to a crisis of confidence in government that persisted long after the conflict ended. The "credibility gap" between the administration's optimistic pronouncements and the reality on the ground eroded public trust in government institutions.

The war also sparked widespread social unrest, particularly on college campuses. The anti-war movement of the 1960s reshaped American youth culture and politics, fostering a skepticism toward authority that would influence a generation.

The financial costs of the war were enormous, contributing to economic challenges in the 1970s and undermining funding for Great Society programs. This guns-versus-butter debate - the tension between military spending and domestic programs - continues to shape budget discussions today.

Perhaps most significantly, the Vietnam War created a reluctance to engage in prolonged overseas military interventions that came to be known as the "Vietnam Syndrome." This shift in foreign policy thinking influenced American strategic decisions for decades.

A Transformative Presidency

Johnson's presidency was transformative in ways both intended and unintended. His domestic achievements reshaped American society, expanding opportunities for millions and establishing government programs that continue to form the backbone of the American social safety net. At the same time, the Vietnam War cast a long shadow over his presidency and the nation. The war's costs - in lives, in money, and in social cohesion - were enormous and long-lasting.

Johnson's presidency offers valuable lessons in the power and limitations of government action. His successes demonstrate how determined leadership can drive sweeping social change. His failures, particularly in Vietnam, serve as a cautionary tale about the unintended consequences of policy decisions and the challenges of projecting power abroad.

The Johnson Era in Perspective

As we look back on the Johnson presidency from our vantage point today, several key themes emerge:

1. The Power of the Presidency: Johnson's tenure demonstrated the enormous potential of presidential leadership to drive social change. His ability to push through major legislation reshaped the country in ways that are still felt today.

2. The Limits of Power: At the same time, the Vietnam War showed the limitations of presidential power, particularly in foreign affairs. Even a skilled politician like Johnson found himself trapped by circumstances and unable to extricate the country from an increasingly unpopular war.

3. The Tension Between Domestic and Foreign Policy: Johnson's experience highlights the ongoing challenge presidents face in balancing domestic priorities with international commitments.

4. The Unintended Consequences of Policy: Many of Johnson's policies had far-reaching effects that weren't fully anticipated at the time. This serves as a reminder of the complexity of governance and the need for careful consideration of potential long-term impacts.

5. The Importance of Timing: Johnson was able to achieve much of his domestic agenda in part because of the unique political circumstances of the mid-1960s. This underscores how the success of a president's agenda often depends on factors beyond their control.

Lessons for Today

Johnson's presidency offers valuable insights for our current political moment. As we face issues of racial justice, economic inequality, healthcare reform, and America's role in the world, the successes and failures of the Johnson era provide important context and lessons.

The civil rights legislation of the 1960s transformed American society, but recent events have shown that the struggle for racial equality is far from over. Johnson's approach - using the full power of the presidency to drive sweeping change - offers one model for addressing systemic inequalities.

The debate over the proper role of government in addressing social issues, a central theme of Johnson's presidency, remains at the heart of many current political disputes. The successes and limitations of Great Society programs continue to inform discussions about how best to address poverty, improve education, and provide healthcare.

In foreign policy, the lessons of Vietnam continue to influence debates over military intervention and America's role in the world. The challenges Johnson faced in balancing international commitments with domestic priorities resonate with more recent presidents who have had to manage overseas conflicts while addressing pressing issues at home.

Part V: Leadership Lessons for Today

1. Crisis Management: Historical Precedents for Modern Challenges

Learning from the Past

As we face the challenges of the 21st century, the leadership of Abraham Lincoln, Lyndon B. Johnson, and the Roosevelts offers valuable insights. These presidents led the nation through some of its darkest hours, from civil war to economic collapse to global conflict. Their approaches to crisis management provide several useful lessons for today's leaders.

Lincoln's Civil War Leadership

Abraham Lincoln faced perhaps the greatest crisis in American history: a nation torn apart by civil war. His leadership during this tumultuous period offers several key lessons:

1. Strong Commitment to Core Principles: Despite enormous pressure, Lincoln never wavered from his commitment to preserve the Union and, eventually, to end slavery. This steadfastness provided a moral compass that guided his decision-making throughout the war.

2. Flexibility in Tactics: While firm in his goals, Lincoln was flexible in his methods. He was willing to try different strategies, change military leaders, and adapt his policies as circumstances changed.

3. Effective Communication: Lincoln's speeches, from the Gettysburg Address to his Second Inaugural, articulated the meaning of the conflict and rallied public support for the war effort. His ability to explain complex issues in simple, powerful language is a model for leaders in any era.

4. Building a Team of Rivals: Lincoln famously included his political opponents in his cabinet, recognizing the value of diverse perspectives in decision-making.

Comparing Lincoln's approach to modern crisis management, we see both similarities and differences. Today's leaders, like Lincoln, must balance firm principles with tactical flexibility. However, the

24-hour news cycle and social media create pressures for instant decision-making that Lincoln didn't face.

FDR and the Great Depression

Franklin D. Roosevelt's handling of the Great Depression offers another set of lessons:

1. Bold Experimentation: FDR's willingness to try new approaches, embodied in his famous quote, "It is common sense to take a method and try it. If it fails, admit it frankly and try another. But above all, try something," is a powerful model for addressing unprecedented challenges.

2. Restoring Confidence: Through his fireside chats and other communications, FDR worked to restore public confidence in the government and the economy. This emphasis on the psychological aspects of crisis management remains relevant today.

3. Comprehensive Approach: The New Deal addressed not just immediate economic needs but also long-term structural issues. This holistic approach to problem-solving is often necessary in complex crises.

4. Building Coalitions: FDR built a broad coalition of support for his policies, bringing together diverse groups under the New Deal banner.

Modern leaders facing economic crises can learn from FDR's approach. The need for clear communication, bold action, and comprehensive solutions remains as relevant today as it was in the 1930s. However, today's global economy adds layers of complexity that FDR didn't have to consider.

LBJ and Civil Rights

Lyndon B. Johnson's leadership during the civil rights era provides lessons in managing social and political crises:

1. Seizing the Moment: Johnson recognized the unique opportunity presented by the civil rights movement and used his political skills to push through landmark legislation.

2. Personal Engagement: Johnson's hands-on approach, including his famous "Johnson Treatment," demonstrates the power of personal persuasion in achieving political goals.

3. Addressing Root Causes: Johnson's War on Poverty sought to address the underlying economic issues fueling social unrest.

4. Legislative Skill: Johnson's mastery of the legislative process allowed him to maneuver through political terrain to achieve his goals.

Today's leaders dealing with social justice issues can learn from Johnson's approach. The need to address both immediate concerns and underlying causes remains crucial. However, the fractured media landscape and increased polarization create new challenges for building consensus.

FDR's Wartime Leadership

Franklin D. Roosevelt's leadership during World War II offers lessons in managing international crises:

1. Building Alliances: FDR's efforts to forge and maintain the Allied coalition demonstrate the importance of international cooperation in addressing global challenges.

2. Strategic Vision: Roosevelt's "Germany First" strategy showed the importance of prioritizing threats and focusing resources where they can have the most impact.

3. Mobilizing National Resources: FDR's leadership in transforming the U.S. economy to support the war effort shows how national crises can require the mobilization of all available resources.

4. Planning for the Future: Even in the midst of war, FDR was planning for the post-war world, as seen in initiatives like the Bretton Woods Conference and the foundation of the United Nations.

Modern leaders facing international crises can draw important lessons from FDR's approach. The need for strong alliances, clear strategic priorities, and long-term planning remains crucial. However, the interconnected global economy and the threat of non-state actors create new challenges that FDR didn't face.

Key Leadership Principles for Managing National Emergencies

Drawing from these historical examples, we can identify several key principles for managing national emergencies:

1. Clear Communication: All four presidents were skilled communicators who could explain complex situations to the public and rally support for their policies. In times of crisis, clear, consistent communication is essential.

2. Adaptability: The ability to adjust strategies in response to changing circumstances was a common trait among these leaders. Flexibility in tactics, while maintaining clear overall goals, is crucial in crisis management.

3. Bold Action: Each of these presidents was willing to take bold, sometimes unprecedented action in response to crises. While careful deliberation is important, crises often require decisive action.

4. Building Coalitions: From Lincoln's Team of Rivals to FDR's New Deal Coalition, these presidents understood the importance of bringing diverse groups together to address national challenges.

5. Long-term Vision: Even while dealing with immediate crises, these leaders kept an eye on the future, implementing policies and institutions that would shape the nation for decades to come.

6. Moral Leadership: Each of these presidents articulated a moral vision that gave meaning to their policies and inspired public support. In times of crisis, people look to leaders not just for practical solutions, but for moral guidance.

7. Learning and Growth: These presidents were willing to learn from their mistakes and grow in office. The ability to acknowledge errors and adjust course is crucial in managing long-term crises.

8. Empathy and Connection: Despite their positions of power, these presidents maintained a connection with ordinary Americans. Their ability to empathize with the struggles of citizens helped them craft policies that addressed real needs.

Applying These Lessons Today

As we face our own national emergencies, from public health crises to economic downturns to social unrest, these historical lessons offer valuable guidance. Today's leaders must operate in a world that differs significantly from that faced by Lincoln,

Johnson, or the Roosevelts. The 24-hour news cycle, social media, global economic interdependence, and the threat of non-state actors all create new challenges.

However, the fundamental principles of crisis leadership remain relevant. Clear communication, adaptability, bold action, coalition-building, long-term vision, moral leadership, continuous learning, and empathy are as important today as they were in the past.

Moreover, studying these historical examples can provide perspective on our current challenges. While our problems may seem unprecedented, looking to the past reminds us that the nation has faced and overcome great challenges before. This historical perspective can provide both guidance and hope as we tackle the crises of our own time.

Crisis management is not just about solving immediate problems, but about using challenging times as opportunities for growth and positive change. Lincoln used the Civil War to end slavery and reshape the nation. FDR used the Great Depression to create a new social contract between government and citizens. Johnson used the turmoil of the 1960s to advance civil rights.

Today's leaders have the opportunity to use our current crises to address long-standing issues and shape a better future. By studying the examples of these great presidents, we can gain insights into how to turn times of trial into moments of transformation.

The lessons of history do not provide easy answers to today's problems. Each generation must find its own solutions to the unique challenges it faces. However, by understanding how great leaders of the past approached national crises, we can gain valuable insights and inspiration for addressing the challenges of our own time.

2. Social Justice: From Emancipation to Contemporary Movements

The Long Arc of Progress

The story of social justice in America is one of slow, often painful progress. From Lincoln's Emancipation Proclamation to today's movements for racial and gender equality, each generation has built upon the achievements of the last, while facing new challenges and setbacks. This chapter traces that evolution, examining how presidential leadership has shaped the nation's journey towards a more just society.

Lincoln and Emancipation

Abraham Lincoln's presidency marked a turning point in the fight for social justice in America. His signing of the Emancipation Proclamation in 1863 was a watershed moment, declaring that all slaves in Confederate states were free. This act, born of both moral conviction and military necessity, set the stage for the eventual abolition of slavery throughout the United States.

Lincoln's approach to emancipation was cautious and pragmatic. He moved slowly, aware of the need to maintain support from border states and Northern Democrats. Yet, his actions were revolutionary in their implications. The 13th Amendment, passed shortly after Lincoln's death, enshrined the abolition of slavery in the Constitution, fundamentally altering the social fabric of the nation.

However, Lincoln's assassination left the work of Reconstruction unfinished. The promise of true equality for freed slaves remained unfulfilled, as Southern states enacted Black Codes and, later, Jim Crow laws to maintain racial segregation and oppression.

The Gilded Age and Progressive Era

The decades following the Civil War saw limited progress in social justice. Presidents of this era, from Grant to McKinley, largely focused on economic development and westward expansion, often at the expense of civil rights. However, the Progressive Era brought renewed attention to social issues. Theodore Roosevelt, while not a strong advocate for racial equality, took steps to address economic injustice. His "Square Deal" policies aimed to balance the interests of business, consumers, and workers. Roosevelt's trust-busting efforts and support for labor reforms laid groundwork for future social justice movements.

The Wilson Paradox

Woodrow Wilson's presidency presents a paradox in the history of social justice. Wilson was a progressive reformer who supported women's suffrage and labor rights. The 19th Amendment, granting women the right to vote, was ratified during his presidency.

Yet, Wilson also oversaw the re-segregation of the federal government and screened the racist film "Birth of a Nation" at the White House. His administration's actions highlight the limitations and contradictions of early 20th century progressivism when it came to racial equality.

FDR and the New Deal

Franklin D. Roosevelt's New Deal marked a significant shift in the federal government's role in promoting social justice. While not primarily focused on racial equality, New Deal programs provided relief and opportunities for many marginalized communities.

FDR's administration included the first "Black Cabinet," a group of African American advisors who helped shape policy. Programs like the Civilian Conservation Corps and the Works Progress Administration, while not free from discrimination, provided jobs and training for many Black Americans.

However, FDR's failure to support anti-lynching legislation and his decision to intern Japanese Americans during World War II demonstrate the limits of his commitment to racial justice.

Truman and Desegregation

Harry Truman took bold steps towards racial equality, desegregating the U.S. military by executive order in 1948. This decision, made in the face of significant opposition, set an important precedent for federal action on civil rights.

Truman also established the President's Committee on Civil Rights, which produced a landmark report, "To Secure These Rights." This report laid out a comprehensive agenda for civil rights reform, much of which would be implemented in the following decades.

Eisenhower and Little Rock

Dwight D. Eisenhower's decision to send federal troops to enforce school desegregation in Little Rock, Arkansas in 1957 was a pivotal moment in civil rights history. While Eisenhower was not an enthusiastic supporter of the civil rights movement, his actions demonstrated the federal government's willingness to intervene to protect civil rights.

The Civil Rights Era

The presidencies of John F. Kennedy and Lyndon B. Johnson saw the most significant advances in civil rights since Reconstruction. Kennedy, initially cautious on civil rights, was pushed to action by events like the Birmingham campaign and the March on Washington.

Johnson, following Kennedy's assassination, used his political skills to push through landmark civil rights legislation. The Civil Rights Act of 1964 and the Voting Rights Act of 1965 outlawed discrimination and removed barriers to voting for African Americans. Johnson's "Great Society" programs also aimed to address poverty and inequality. However, his escalation of the Vietnam War diverted resources and attention from these domestic initiatives.

Nixon and the Southern Strategy

Richard Nixon's presidency saw a shift in approach to civil rights. While his administration continued to enforce civil rights laws and implemented affirmative action policies, Nixon also employed the "Southern Strategy," appealing to white Southern voters opposed to civil rights advances.

This strategy marked the beginning of a realignment in American politics, with the Republican Party becoming increasingly aligned with opposition to civil rights reforms.

The Reagan Era and Backlash

Ronald Reagan's presidency represented a backlash against the civil rights advances of previous decades. His administration opposed affirmative action and sought to roll back many Great Society programs. However, Reagan also signed legislation creating Martin Luther King Jr. Day as a federal holiday, demonstrating the complicated nature of presidential influence on social justice issues.

Clinton and "Don't Ask, Don't Tell"

Bill Clinton's presidency saw mixed progress on social justice issues. His "Don't Ask, Don't Tell" policy, while intended as a compromise, effectively codified discrimination against LGBTQ+ individuals in the military. However, Clinton also appointed record numbers of women and minorities to government positions.

Obama and the Symbolism of Progress

Barack Obama's election as the first African American president was itself a milestone in the long struggle for racial equality. Obama's presidency saw significant advances in LGBTQ+ rights, including the repeal of "Don't Ask, Don't Tell" and the legalization of same-sex marriage.

However, Obama's tenure also saw the rise of new civil rights challenges, including police violence against Black Americans and the emergence of the Black Lives Matter movement.

Trump and the Backlash to Progress

Donald Trump's presidency represented another backlash against civil rights advances. His administration rolled back protections for LGBTQ+ individuals, implemented restrictive immigration policies, and often used divisive rhetoric on racial issues.

However, Trump's presidency also sparked renewed activism, leading to large-scale protests and increased engagement in the political process among marginalized communities.

Biden and Contemporary Movements

Joe Biden's presidency has seen efforts to address racial equity and LGBTQ+ rights, including executive orders on racial equity and transgender rights in the military. However, challenges remain, including ongoing racial disparities in health care, education, and criminal justice.

The Ongoing Struggle

The evolution of social justice in America from Lincoln to the present day reveals a pattern of progress and backlash. Each advance has been met with resistance, yet the overall trend has been towards greater equality and inclusion.

Presidential leadership has played a crucial role in this progress. From Lincoln's Emancipation Proclamation to Johnson's Civil Rights Act to Obama's support for same-sex marriage, presidents have used their platform and power to advance social justice causes.

However, presidential action alone has never been sufficient. Progress has always depended on the work of activists, organizers, and ordinary citizens pushing for change. The most effective presidents have been those who could harness and channel this grassroots energy into concrete policy changes.

Lessons for Today

As we face contemporary social justice challenges, several lessons emerge from this historical overview:

1. The power of presidential rhetoric: From Lincoln's "new birth of freedom" to Johnson's "We Shall Overcome," presidential words can inspire and mobilize.

2. The importance of timing: Successful presidents have seized moments of crisis or public attention to push for reforms.

3. The need for persistence: Progress on social justice issues often takes decades, spanning multiple administrations.

4. The value of coalition-building: Presidents who have achieved lasting change have built broad coalitions of support.

5. The ongoing nature of the struggle: Each generation faces new challenges and must renew the fight for equality and justice.

Today's movements for racial justice, gender equality, and LGBTQ+ rights are part of a long American tradition. They build on past achievements while addressing new and ongoing inequities. The lessons of presidential leadership on social justice issues offer both inspiration and practical guidance for continuing this vital work.

3. Economic Challenges: Addressing Inequality

The Persistent Problem of Economic Disparity

Economic inequality has been a recurring challenge throughout American history. From the Gilded Age to the Great Depression, from the postwar boom to today's widening wealth gap, presidents have battled with how to create a more equitable economy. This chapter examines how past leaders approached this issue and what lessons we can draw for our current economic challenges.

Lincoln's Vision: A Fair Chance for All

Abraham Lincoln's economic philosophy centered on providing opportunity for all Americans. His support for the Homestead Act of 1862, which offered public land to settlers, aimed to give ordinary citizens a chance at economic independence. Lincoln believed that a system that allowed people to benefit from their own labor would create a more just and prosperous society.

Lincoln's approach to economic inequality was rooted in his own experiences of poverty and hard work. He saw the government's role as creating conditions for individuals to improve their lot through their own efforts, rather than directly redistributing wealth.

Today, Lincoln's ideas might translate into policies that focus on education, job training, and creating opportunities for entrepreneurship. The principle of giving people the tools to succeed remains relevant in our discussions about economic mobility.

Theodore Roosevelt: The Trust-Buster

Theodore Roosevelt's presidency marked a shift towards more active government intervention in the economy. Faced with the rise of powerful monopolies, Roosevelt used antitrust laws to break up large corporations he saw as stifling competition and harming consumers.

Roosevelt's "Square Deal" sought to balance the interests of businesses, workers, and consumers. He supported labor rights, pushed for consumer protections, and advocated for conservation of natural resources. His approach recognized that unchecked corporate power could lead to economic inequalities that threatened the health of democracy.

In our current era of large tech companies and concerns about market concentration, Roosevelt's trust-busting efforts offer insights into how the government can promote competition and protect consumer interests.

FDR and the New Deal: Rewriting the Rules

Franklin D. Roosevelt's response to the Great Depression represented the most sweeping attempt to address economic inequality in American history up to that point. The New Deal fundamentally altered the relationship between government, business, and citizens.

Key elements of FDR's approach included:

1. Direct Relief: Programs like the Works Progress Administration provided jobs for the unemployed.

2. Social Safety Net: The creation of Social Security established a basic level of economic security for the elderly.

3. Labor Rights: The Wagner Act protected workers' right to unionize, helping to boost wages and improve working conditions.

4. Financial Regulation: New rules for banks and stock markets aimed to prevent the kind of speculation that led to the 1929 crash.

5. Progressive Taxation: Higher taxes on the wealthy helped fund new government programs.

FDR's policies were based on the principle that the government had a responsibility to ensure a basic level of economic security for all citizens. This idea continues to shape debates about the role of government in the economy.

LBJ's War on Poverty: Addressing Root Causes

Lyndon B. Johnson's Great Society programs represented another major effort to combat economic inequality. Johnson saw poverty as a systemic problem that required comprehensive solutions.

Key initiatives included:

1. Education: Programs like Head Start aimed to give disadvantaged children a better start in life.

2. Healthcare: The creation of Medicare and Medicaid expanded access to healthcare for the elderly and poor.

3. Job Training: Programs like the Job Corps sought to provide skills to unemployed youth.

4. Community Development: The Model Cities program aimed to improve urban areas and create economic opportunities.

Johnson's approach recognized the interconnected nature of economic challenges, linking issues like education, healthcare, and housing to overall economic well-being. This holistic view of economic inequality remains relevant today.

Reagan's Supply-Side Economics: A Different Approach

Ronald Reagan's presidency marked a significant shift in approach to economic policy. Reagan argued that reducing taxes and regulations would stimulate economic growth, ultimately benefiting all Americans through a "trickle-down" effect.

Key elements of Reagan's economic policy included:

1. Tax Cuts: Significant reductions in income tax rates, especially for high earners.

2. Deregulation: Removing government regulations on various industries.

3. Reduced Social Spending: Cuts to many social programs established under the New Deal and Great Society.

Reagan's approach was based on the idea that a rising tide lifts all boats - that overall economic growth would reduce inequality more effectively than direct government intervention. This philosophy continues to influence conservative economic thinking today.

Clinton's "Third Way": Balancing Growth and Equity

Bill Clinton attempted to chart a middle course between traditional liberal and conservative economic approaches. His "Third Way" sought to promote economic growth while also addressing inequality.

Key policies included:

1. Welfare Reform: Changes to the welfare system aimed to encourage work.

2. Earned Income Tax Credit Expansion: This policy effectively raised incomes for low-wage workers.

3. Minimum Wage Increases: Clinton signed into law two minimum wage hikes.

4. Free Trade Agreements: Policies like NAFTA aimed to boost overall economic growth.

Clinton's approach attempted to balance promoting economic growth with providing support for lower-income Americans. The tension between these goals remains a central challenge in addressing economic inequality.

Obama's Response to the Great Recession

Barack Obama's presidency was defined by the response to the 2008 financial crisis and its aftermath. His approach combined elements of FDR's interventionism with more market-oriented policies.

Key elements included:

1. Stimulus Package: The American Recovery and Reinvestment Act aimed to boost economic growth and create jobs.

2. Healthcare Reform: The Affordable Care Act expanded access to health insurance.

3. Financial Regulation: The Dodd-Frank Act imposed new rules on the financial industry.

4. Progressive Taxation: Obama allowed Bush-era tax cuts for high earners to expire.

Obama's policies reflected a belief that the government has a role in both stimulating economic growth and ensuring that its benefits are widely shared. His approach to inequality focused on expanding access to healthcare and education while also implementing more progressive taxation.

Trump's Tax Cuts and Deregulation

Donald Trump's economic policies in many ways represented a return to Reagan-era supply-side economics. His approach centered on the belief that cutting taxes and regulations would spur economic growth.

Key elements included:

1. Tax Cuts: The 2017 Tax Cuts and Jobs Act significantly reduced corporate tax rates and taxes for high earners.

2. Deregulation: Rollback of many Obama-era regulations, particularly in the environmental sphere.

3. Trade Policy: Use of tariffs and renegotiation of trade agreements aimed to protect American industries.

Trump argued that his policies would lead to job creation and wage growth that would benefit all Americans. Critics contended that the benefits primarily accrued to corporations and wealthy individuals.

Biden's Build Back Better: A New New Deal?

Joe Biden's economic agenda represents an attempt to address inequality through large-scale government investment and more progressive taxation. His approach in many ways harkens back to FDR's New Deal and LBJ's Great Society.

Key proposals include:

1. Infrastructure Investment: Large-scale spending on roads, bridges, and green energy projects.

2. Education and Childcare: Expanded access to early childhood education and affordable childcare.

3. Healthcare: Proposals to expand Medicare and reduce prescription drug costs.

4. Progressive Taxation: Proposed increases in taxes on corporations and high earners.

Biden's policies reflect a belief that addressing inequality requires both "top-down" approaches like progressive taxation and "bottom-up" investments in education, healthcare, and infrastructure.

Enduring Economic Principles

Looking at these various approaches to economic inequality, several enduring principles emerge:

1. The Importance of Opportunity: From Lincoln's Homestead Act to modern education policies, creating opportunities for economic advancement has been a consistent theme.

2. The Debate Over Government's Role: The tension between those who favor more active government intervention and those who prefer market-based solutions has been a constant in American economic policy.

3. The Connection Between Growth and Equity: Presidents have worked to balance promoting overall economic growth with ensuring its benefits are widely shared.

4. The Power of Taxation: Tax policy has been a key tool for addressing inequality, from FDR's progressive taxation to Reagan's tax cuts.

5. The Importance of Education and Skills: Improving education and job skills has been a consistent strategy for addressing economic inequality.

6. The Role of Labor Rights: From FDR's support for unions to modern debates about the minimum wage, workers' rights have been central to discussions of economic fairness.

7. The Impact of Technological Change: Each era has had to battle with how technological advancements affect economic inequality.

Lessons for Today

As we face our own challenges of economic inequality, including wage stagnation, the impact of automation, and the concentration of wealth, these historical approaches offer valuable insights:

1. Comprehensive Solutions: The most effective approaches to inequality have addressed multiple factors, from education to healthcare to labor rights.

2. Balancing Growth and Equity: Successful policies have found ways to promote overall economic growth while ensuring its benefits are widely shared.

3. Adapting to Changing Circumstances: Each era has required new solutions tailored to its specific economic challenges.

4. The Power of Presidential Leadership: Presidents have played a key role in shaping the national conversation about economic fairness and mobilizing support for their policies.

The experiences of past presidents provide both inspiration and cautionary tales. They remind us that while the specific challenges may change, the fundamental questions about how to create a fair and prosperous economy for all Americans remain constant.

4. America's Global Role: Lessons from Four Presidencies

The Evolution of American Foreign Policy

The presidencies of Abraham Lincoln, Lyndon B. Johnson, Theodore Roosevelt, and Franklin D. Roosevelt each marked significant shifts in America's role on the world stage. From the Civil War to World War II, these leaders addressed major international challenges, shaping the nation's foreign policy and its global standing. Their approaches offer valuable insights for addressing current international issues.

Lincoln: Preserving the Union, Shaping Global Democracy

While Abraham Lincoln's presidency was dominated by domestic concerns, his leadership during the Civil War had profound international implications. Lincoln's primary foreign policy goal was to prevent European powers, particularly Britain and France, from recognizing or supporting the Confederacy.

Lincoln's diplomatic strategy included:

1. Framing the war as a struggle for democracy and union, rather than just about slavery, to appeal to European liberals.
2. Using economic leverage, such as cotton diplomacy, to influence European decision-making.
3. Employing skilled diplomats like Charles Francis Adams to represent American interests abroad.

Lincoln's success in keeping European powers out of the Civil War was a significant diplomatic achievement. Moreover, the Union's victory helped solidify the United States as a major world power and served as an inspiration for democratic movements globally.

Lessons for Today:

1. The power of moral leadership in international affairs
2. The importance of skilled diplomacy in crisis situations
3. The interplay between domestic policy and foreign relations

Theodore Roosevelt: America as a Global Power

Theodore Roosevelt's presidency marked America's emergence as a global power. His foreign policy was characterized by assertive diplomacy backed by military strength, encapsulated in his famous quote, "Speak softly and carry a big stick."

Key aspects of Roosevelt's foreign policy included:

1. The Roosevelt Corollary to the Monroe Doctrine, asserting America's right to intervene in Latin American affairs
2. Mediating the end of the Russo-Japanese War, for which he won the Nobel Peace Prize
3. The construction of the Panama Canal, significantly enhancing America's naval power

Roosevelt believed in American exceptionalism and saw the United States as having a responsibility to play an active role in world affairs. He sought to balance power politics with ethical considerations, as seen in his efforts to promote peace and his advocacy for international arbitration.

Lessons for Today:

1. The balance between diplomacy and military strength

2. The role of great powers in maintaining international order

3. The potential for American leadership in conflict resolution

Franklin D. Roosevelt: From Isolationism to Global Leadership

Franklin D. Roosevelt's presidency spanned a critical period in American foreign policy, from the isolationism of the 1930s to America's emergence as a superpower after World War II.

FDR's foreign policy evolution included:

1. Early focus on domestic issues during the Great Depression

2. Gradual shift towards interventionism as global threats increased

3. Lend-Lease program to support Allied powers before U.S. entry into WWII

4. Leadership of the Allied war effort

5. Vision for post-war international order, including the United Nations

FDR's approach was characterized by pragmatism and a willingness to work with diverse allies to achieve American objectives. He recognized the interconnectedness of global affairs and the need for American leadership in shaping the post-war world.

Lessons for Today:

1. The importance of adaptability in foreign policy
2. The value of international institutions in maintaining peace
3. The role of economic aid as a tool of foreign policy

Lyndon B. Johnson: Cold War Challenges and Vietnam

Lyndon B. Johnson's foreign policy was dominated by Cold War considerations and the escalating conflict in Vietnam. While Johnson preferred to focus on domestic issues, global events demanded much of his attention.

Key aspects of Johnson's foreign policy included:

1. Escalation of U.S. involvement in Vietnam
2. Containment of communism as a guiding principle
3. Efforts to promote development in Third World countries
4. Management of relations with the Soviet Union, including arms control negotiations

Johnson's presidency illustrates the challenges of balancing domestic and foreign policy priorities. His experiences in Vietnam also highlight the potential pitfalls of military interventions and the importance of clear, achievable objectives in foreign engagements.

Lessons for Today:

1. The risks of mission creep in military interventions
2. The impact of foreign policy decisions on domestic politics
3. The challenges of maintaining public support for prolonged conflicts

Enduring Principles in American Foreign Policy

Examining these four presidencies reveals several enduring principles in American foreign policy:

1. The tension between isolationism and interventionism
2. The use of both hard and soft power in pursuing national interests
3. The role of American values and ideals in shaping foreign policy
4. The importance of building and maintaining alliances

5. The interplay between domestic politics and foreign policy decisions

These principles continue to shape American foreign policy today, as leaders face issues ranging from global terrorism to climate change to shifting power dynamics among world powers.

Applying Historical Lessons to Current Challenges

1. Managing Relations with Rising Powers

The rise of China as a global power presents challenges similar to those faced by Theodore Roosevelt in dealing with emerging nations of his time. Roosevelt's approach of balanced engagement - maintaining military strength while seeking diplomatic solutions - offers a potential model for managing this relationship.

2. Addressing Global Crises

FDR's leadership during World War II demonstrates the potential for American leadership in addressing global crises. His ability to build coalitions and mobilize national resources could inform approaches to issues like climate change or global health crises.

3. Balancing Interventionism and Restraint

The contrasting approaches of Theodore Roosevelt's assertive foreign policy and the initial isolationism of FDR's early years highlight the ongoing debate about America's proper role in world affairs. This tension is evident in current debates about military interventions and international commitments.

4. Promoting Democracy and Human Rights

Lincoln's framing of the Civil War as a struggle for democracy resonates with ongoing debates about the role of values in American foreign policy. His approach suggests the potential power of moral leadership on the world stage.

5. Managing Long-term Conflicts

Johnson's experience in Vietnam offers cautionary lessons about the risks of open-ended military commitments. These lessons could inform strategies for managing ongoing conflicts and military engagements.

6. Building International Institutions

FDR's vision for the United Nations reflects a belief in the importance of international institutions in maintaining global order. This approach remains relevant in addressing transnational challenges that require multilateral cooperation.

7. Economic Diplomacy

From Lincoln's cotton diplomacy to FDR's Lend-Lease program, these presidents recognized the power of economic tools in achieving foreign policy objectives. This principle continues to be relevant in an era of global economic interdependence.

Challenges for Modern Leaders

Today's leaders face a world that is in many ways more complex than that encountered by Lincoln, the Roosevelts, or Johnson. Rapid technological change, the threat of non-state actors, and global challenges like climate change create new foreign policy imperatives.

However, the fundamental questions faced by these earlier presidents remain relevant:

1. How can America use its power responsibly and effectively?
2. How should we balance our values with our interests in foreign policy?
3. What is the proper balance between domestic and foreign policy priorities?
4. How can we build and maintain effective international coalitions?

5. What is the appropriate use of military force in achieving foreign policy objectives?

The experiences of these four presidents offer valuable insights. They remind us of the power of American leadership when exercised wisely, the importance of diplomacy and coalition-building, and the need for a clear vision in guiding foreign policy.

The lessons from these presidencies also highlight the importance of adaptability in foreign policy. Each of these leaders had to adjust their approaches in response to changing global circumstances. This flexibility, combined with a clear sense of national purpose, allowed them to address international challenges.

Moreover, these presidents demonstrated the importance of effective communication in foreign policy. From Lincoln's careful framing of the Civil War to FDR's fireside chats explaining America's role in World War II, these leaders understood the need to build public support for their foreign policy initiatives.

In the face of our own crossroads in foreign policy, with debates about America's role in a changing world order, the examples of these presidents provide both inspiration and caution. They remind us of America's potential to be a force for good in the world, while also highlighting the risks and challenges inherent in global engagement.

Conclusion: The Enduring Legacy of Presidential Leadership

Reflecting on the presidencies of Abraham Lincoln, Lyndon B. Johnson, Theodore Roosevelt, and Franklin D. Roosevelt, we see how their leadership continues to shape American politics and inform our approach to national challenges. These four leaders, each facing monumental crises, offer enduring lessons in governance, vision, and the art of leadership.

As we face contemporary challenges like climate change, economic inequality, technological disruption, and global instability, the examples of these presidents offer both inspiration and practical guidance. They remind us that with vision, courage, and skillful leadership, America can overcome even the most daunting obstacles.

The presidency, shaped by these four leaders, stands as a powerful force for national renewal and progress. Their legacies continue to influence policy debates, shape our institutions, and inspire new generations to public service. While the challenges we face may differ, the core qualities they exemplified - courage, vision, empathy, and an unyielding commitment to democratic values - remain as relevant as ever.

Moving forward, we carry with us the lessons of these remarkable leaders. Their stories not only provide a roadmap for handling the challenges of our era but also reaffirm the potential of American leadership to shape a better future for all.

The End.